"Josie, I'm thinking that you and I could make a new start together.

"I want to do the very best I can for my family. I want to make up to them for what I've put them through. You're so good with my daughters."

A new start somewhere else? Her mind shot back to those words. "What are you saying?"

"I would be honored if you would marry me and come to Colorado with us," he said.

The night sounds faded into the silent cocoon of her whirling mind and his words took over her thinking. Astonishment stole her breath. Marry him? He'd asked her to marry him?

He was handsome and smart. She'd witnessed his tenderness toward his children, listened to his strong words of love as he preached straight from the Word of God. This imposing and fascinating man sitting on her porch had proposed to her!

D0595906

Books by Cheryl St.John

Love Inspired Historical

The Preacher's Wife

Harlequin Historical

Rain Shadow	*The Tenderfoot Bride*
Heaven Can Wait	*Prairie Wife*
Land of Dreams	*His Secondhand Wife*
Saint or Sinner	*Wed Under Western Skies*
Badlands Bride	"Almost a Bride"
The Mistaken Widow	*The Lawman's Bride*
Joe's Wife	*The Preacher's Daughter*
The Doctor's Wife	*A Western Winter Wonderland*
Sweet Annie	"Christmas Day Family"
The Gunslinger's Bride	*The Magic of Christmas*
Christmas Gold	"A Baby Blue Christmas"
"Colorado Wife"	*Her Montana Man*

CHERYL ST.JOHN

A peacemaker, a romantic, an idealist and a discouraged perfectionist are the terms that Cheryl uses to describe herself. The award-winning author of both historical and contemporary novels says she's been told that she is painfully honest.

Cheryl admits to being an avid collector, displaying everything from dolls to depression glass, as well as white ironstone, teapots, cups and saucers, old photographs and—most especially—books. When not doing a home-improvement project, she and her husband love to browse antique shops. In her spare time, she's an amateur photographer and a pretty good baker.

She says that knowing her stories bring hope and pleasure to readers is one of the best parts of being a writer. The other wonderful part is being able to set her own schedule and have time to work around her growing family.

Cheryl loves to hear from readers! E-mail her at: SaintJohn@aol.com.

The Preacher's Wife

CHERYL ST.JOHN

Steeple
Hill®

Published by Steeple Hill Books™

If you purchased this book without a cover you should be aware that this book is stolen property. It was reported as "unsold and destroyed" to the publisher, and neither the author nor the publisher has received any payment for this "stripped book."

STEEPLE HILL BOOKS

Steeple
Hill®

Recycling programs
for this product may
not exist in your area.

ISBN-13: 978-0-373-82813-5

THE PREACHER'S WIFE

Copyright © 2009 by Cheryl Ludwigs

All rights reserved. Except for use in any review, the reproduction or utilization of this work in whole or in part in any form by any electronic, mechanical or other means, now known or hereafter invented, including xerography, photocopying and recording, or in any information storage or retrieval system, is forbidden without the written permission of the editorial office, Steeple Hill Books, 233 Broadway, New York, NY 10279 U.S.A.

This is a work of fiction, Names, characters, places and incidents are either the product of the author's imagination or are used fictitiously, and any resemblance to actual persons, living or dead, business establishments, events or locales is entirely coincidental.

This edition published by arrangement with Steeple Hill Books.

® and TM are trademarks of Steeple Hill Books, used under license. Trademarks indicated with ® are registered in the United States Patent and Trademark Office, the Canadian Trade Marks Office and in other countries.

www.SteepleHill.com

Printed in U.S.A.

So shall my word be that goeth forth out of my mouth; it shall not return unto me void, but it shall accomplish that which I please, and it shall prosper in the thing whereto I sent it. For ye shall go out with joy, and be led forth with peace: the mountains and the hills shall break forth before you into singing, and all the trees of the field will clap their hands.

—*Isaiah* 55:11–12

With love and appreciation I dedicate this book to my mentor, teacher, pastor, prayer partner, painting buddy and friend, Betty Jo Marples. Special lady, you give one hundred percent of yourself to all you do and to everyone who knows you. Whether I need a listening ear, an advocate or someone to tell me the straight truth, I can depend on you. Your example encourages me to look at others through the eyes of Jesus. You always see the best in me, believe the best for me, and expect the best from me. Thank you, friend.

Chapter One

Durham, Nebraska, June 1869

Only her husband's physical body lay beneath the lush grass in the fenced-in cemetery behind the tiny white church. His spirit had gone on to be with the Lord, but her mother-in-law insisted that Sunday afternoons were for paying respects to the dead. Josephine Randolph knelt and pulled a fledgling weed from beside the flat piece of granite engraved with her husband's name.

Margaretta slipped a lace-edged hankie from the hidden pocket of her emerald-green dress and dabbed her eyes. "He was too young," she said for the thousandth time. "Too young to lose his life."

Josie nodded. It had been three years, and while she had mourned her husband's death and missed his company, there were no tears left. She had loved him. She had been a good wife. But in his affections she had always taken second place to her mother-in-law. She hastened to remind herself that losing a son or daughter was devastating. Margaretta had lost her only child. Of course the woman was still suffering.

"It would be easier if I could take comfort in the fact that he'd left behind a living legacy."

Knowing and dreading what was coming next, Josie got up and brushed her palms together.

Margaretta sniffed into her hankie. "Your inability to give me a grandchild is almost more than I can bear."

Josie turned her gaze to the countryside, spotted an orange and black butterfly and watched it flutter on the breeze as she steeled herself.

"A child would have been a part of him I could hold on to. If only right now I could be caring for a little boy or girl with Bram's features. I would have so loved to watch him grow. His child would have been such a comfort to me."

Josie wanted to cry, too. She wanted to rail at the woman who made her feel every inch as insignificant as her son had. Didn't Margaretta think a child would have been a comfort to her, as well? Didn't she know that Josie's loneliness was eating her up on the inside? Didn't she think Josie wanted more out of life than…than…*this?*

Momentarily, she closed her eyes against the painfully blue summer sky. She'd never wanted anything more than a family of her own. She'd spent her entire childhood waiting for her circuit-judge father to return home. The times he had, he'd spared her only meager attention before leaving again.

Because Bram Randolph had been a local newspaperman, she'd known he wouldn't be a traveler. She'd married him with the hope of a secure future. Time had proven Bram more concerned with the whims of Margaretta than the needs of his young wife, however. And that was the simple fact.

"You *are* coming to the house for dinner, aren't you?"

And be exposed to yet another opportunity for Margaretta to pursue her weekly harangue about Josie's barrenness? Josie opened her eyes. "I'm fixing a stew for Reverend Martin," she replied matter-of-factly. "I'll stay and keep him company."

"He seems to be recovering well." Margaretta smoothed the fingers of her beaded gloves. "Whatever you're doing must be working."

Josie managed a smile. "God's doing His part, too."

Margaretta gathered the hem of her voluminous skirt and walked across the thick spring grass toward the street.

Josie glanced down and read the headstone again. "Beloved son and husband." Not father. Sometimes she felt so incomplete, so alone. She hadn't given her husband children, and for that glaring inadequacy, Margaretta would never forgive her.

"Have a good afternoon!" she called after the woman.

Margaretta delivered a tepid wave and continued marching toward her home a few blocks away. Josie experienced the same relief she always did when her obligatory mourning session and weekly dressing-down was over. At least she'd had a good reason to forgo lengthening the torment by joining the woman for a meal. Margaretta's house had a cold, depressing atmosphere that matched the woman's attitude.

Josie glanced at the bright blue sky with a longing that was rising up so swift and strong that the ache took her breath away. She'd prayed for contentment, but she needed more than this. When she didn't keep busy enough, she daydreamed of impossible things....

Taking a deep breath, Josie made her way with renewed purpose to the shaded two-story house beside the church. She climbed the back porch steps and let herself in. She'd started a stew earlier, and now checked the savory broth, adding water and salt.

"It's Josie!" she called, removing her bonnet and sweeping along the hallway toward the front of the house.

"Who else would be banging pans in my kitchen?" came the good-natured reply.

She found Reverend Martin in his study, seated where she'd left him, on an overstuffed chair with a plaid wool blanket tucked around his legs. He closed his Bible and removed his spectacles, setting both aside. Last March he'd fallen from the roof of the church while replacing shingles, and had broken several bones, including his collarbone and ribs. A particularly severe break in his leg had become infected, and he'd been bedridden with a fever for weeks. Eventually he'd recovered, and was only now able to move from his bed to the study. The town doctor said it would likely be several more weeks before he'd be strong enough to resume his duties.

She'd always considered him a mentor, but these past weeks had made them friends, as well. "The fire's died down," she said. "I'll get a few logs."

"I can't seem to get warm." He was paler and thinner than before the accident, and the change in such a vital, life-loving man was heartbreaking. The man was probably only in his late thirties, but these past weeks had taken a toll. Josie had dedicated herself to seeing him recover to his former self.

"The stew will warm you from the inside out," she assured him. She took two split logs from the box beside the fireplace and knelt to add them to the fire, then used the poker to adjust the wood until the flames caught and licked up around the sides. The bark snapped in the blaze. Warmth spread from the hearth to where the reverend was sitting.

"That's nice," he said with a grateful smile. "I barely have time to realize a need before you've seen to it."

"It's a privilege to help."

"And a help you are. I don't know what I would do without you."

"God would send someone. But I was available."

He chuckled. "You're a woman of great faith, Josie, but you count yourself a little short."

She seated herself on a nearby ottoman.

"A lot of people are available," he told her. "Few are willing."

She never doubted that God was taking care of the reverend. It was when she thought of her own needs that her confidence got a little shaky. "How about a game of checkers before dinner?" she asked.

He gave her a mock frown and flicked his hand as though shooing away a fly. "Do you think I enjoy your kings chasing my last disk around the board, delaying the inevitable?"

She laughed. "Oh, come now. You win sometimes."

"Only if you feel particularly sorry for me and deliberately pass up chances to jump. We need a new game, one I have a hope of winning."

"Based on chance, rather than skill, Reverend?"

"Didn't I see you and James setting up the board the other evening?"

James, a fatherless lad of about fourteen, came by a few times a week to split wood and perform a few other chores. Josie had quickly sensed that, because his mother worked evenings at the café, James was lonely. She'd offered to teach him the game. "You did. He's fast becoming an apt opponent."

The reverend's enormous calico leaped from its spot on the divan to run through the doorway into the nearest bedroom.

"Must be a caller," the reverend said.

Most everyone knocked at the back door and then walked in, but a rap sounded at the front. Josie and the reverend exchanged a puzzled glance before she got up.

A broad-shouldered man in a brown hat and buckskin jacket stood in the dappled sunlight that filtered through the leaves of the twin maple trees. She had a sudden, swift impression of troubled intensity as his gaze bored into hers.

"Good afternoon, sir," Josie greeted him.

He removed his hat, revealing thick chestnut hair in need of a cut. "Ma'am," he said in greeting. "I'm Samuel Hart. The preacher sent by the First Christian Alliance."

Behind him, three girls of varying ages waited in the street near a dusty team attached to a canvas-covered wagon.

His name registered immediately. "Of course! Come in."

He turned and summoned the girls, the fringe of his jacket swaying as he gestured. The girls she assumed were his daughters were wearing clean but wrinkled clothing, and their hair was neatly tucked beneath stiff-brimmed bonnets.

He handed her his hat, still warm from his head, and she laid it on the hall table before ushering the little troupe into the study. "The interim preacher is here," she said.

Samuel strode forward and shook the elder man's

hand. His size and his sun-darkened face and hands made the reverend seem even sicklier in comparison. "Pleased to meet you, sir. These are my daughters. Elisabeth."

Elisabeth was the tallest and oldest, with blue eyes and a full face. Her weary smile was hesitant.

"Abigail." The middle daughter had hair a paler blond than the other two, blue eyes, a narrow face and a prominent chin.

"And Anna." The youngest of the trio possessed wide hazel eyes and a charming smattering of freckles.

A look of confusion wrinkled Reverend Martin's brow. "Josie, didn't the letters say that Samuel was traveling with his wife and family?"

Josie had recalled the same thing. Before she could answer, Samuel Hart said, "My wife died on the way."

The snapping fire was the only sound for a moment.

Anna slipped her hand into Abigail's and the three girls huddled closer, their expressions somber, the pain of their loss evident.

"I'm deeply sorry," Reverend Martin said.

Samuel nodded curtly, the subject apparently closed.

"This is Josephine Randolph." The reverend indicated Josie with a nod. "God sent her to me. She cooks, takes care of the house, does my laundry—she even handled my bills and mail while I was laid up."

"Pleased to make your acquaintance, ma'am."

It was inappropriate that she should notice his well-defined cheekbones or his recently shaved, firm, square chin, but she had. Even his deep, rich voice arrested her attention. But his eyes…she'd never seen so much suffering in a person's eyes, and the sight carved a confusing ache inside her chest.

Samuel turned his gaze to look pointedly at his daughters.

One at a time, they said, "Pleased to meet you."

Glad for the distraction, she said, "You've arrived just in time for dinner. I trust you're hungry. Would you like to help me make biscuits?"

"*I* would," Abigail said with a bright smile.

Watching his daughters' hesitation and discomfort pained Sam. He hoped the pretty young woman's friendly welcome made this day a trifle easier than the rest. The past weeks had been grueling, both physically and emotionally. "All of you will help Mrs. Randolph," he called after them.

Over her shoulder, Anna cast him a wide-eyed glance, her expression so much like his late wife's that it made his breath hitch in his chest.

Reverend Martin indicated the settee. "Have a seat."

Sam brought his attention to their meeting and to the minister for whom he would temporarily be substituting. He was probably about ten years older than Sam.

Taking the offered seat, Sam was glad they'd

stopped outside town to wash up and put on clean clothing. The man's home was plain, but tastefully furnished and spotlessly clean.

"I understand you had a setback in your recovery," Sam began.

"I was busted up pretty bad," Henry answered with a nod. "Collarbone was the most painful. Couldn't do anything for myself. My leg was on the mend, but then I got an infection. The doc told me he considered taking it off, but he and Josie came up with a plan for medicine and poultices. The other women took turns staying with her, but she was here day and night through the worst of it. She's a praying woman, that Josie. Has God's ear, too, she does. I can walk on my leg now, but it's almighty weak." He grimaced in exasperation. "Like the rest of me. Kind of lost my gumption."

"That's why the Alliance sent me," Sam assured him. "I'll be here to help you with your duties for the next several weeks."

The First Christian Alliance had offered Sam a church in Colorado. It had always been his dream to travel westward, so he'd leaped at the prospect. At the time, it had seemed like a glorious opportunity. This assignment was a chance he hadn't been willing to miss, so they'd sold their home and packed their belongings.

Meanwhile, they learned of this small congregation in Nebraska that needed someone to fill in while their regular minister recuperated. Sam had set out filled with so much hope and expectancy. He'd embraced the physical challenges of the trip with the enthusiasm of a man running toward his dream. Crossing wide-open country and testing his skills with a wagon and team and rifle was an unparalleled prospect for adventure.

How naive he'd been. He'd walked his unprepared family right into danger, and he'd been unable to protect them.

"I'm sorry about your wife." Henry's tone held sympathy, his kind expression an opening to talk.

Sam hadn't voiced the burden on his heart. He had to be strong and push on. He'd started this, and he couldn't let his children down. He would see this through.

He looked into the other man's eyes and swallowed hard. The weight that had been pressing on Sam's chest sent out a new arrow of pain, and he was weary of holding himself together. "My wife and daughters were thrown from our wagon as we were crossing a river last April. My wife drowned."

My wife drowned. Simple words that didn't begin to explain the ghastly choice he'd been forced to make. It didn't reflect the horror of watching Carrie being washed downstream in a muddy torrent, or of his frantic haste to rescue his daughters and search for his wife.

He couldn't close his eyes at night without remembering the echoing gunfire that had drawn him to where one of the men stood in the shallows. He never woke up without seeing his wife limp and pale, her hair snagged in tree roots. More than anything, he wanted to remember her the way she'd been, but it was her pale, lifeless image that tortured him.

"The wagon righted itself and the team pulled it on across," he said. "Didn't even lose a bag of flour or a wooden bucket." The irony was eating a hole in his gut.

Mrs. Kennedy and another woman had laid out his wife in her finest Sunday dress, a blue one with tiny sprigs of white flowers and lace cuffs. With his heart an aching cavity in his chest, Sam had removed her wedding ring and given it to Elisabeth.

He'd second-guessed himself hundreds of times over the past days and nights, questioned his wisdom in bringing his family west, doubted his choices the day Carrie had died. Elisabeth had been six feet away; Carrie had been twenty or more. He'd shouted for the other men to find Carrie while he rescued his daughters.

What if he'd let the others get the girls and he'd ridden along the bank while he'd still been able to locate her? What if he'd let Abigail cling to that branch until one of the others got to her and had instead taken those precious minutes to find his wife?

The constant examination was pointless. His head told him that regret wouldn't change anything, but the thoughts plagued him all the same. His lofty plans mocked him.

His children were motherless and he was a widower. If he hadn't wanted to come west they would still be living in their comfortable house in Philadelphia. The girls would be in school now and Carrie would be singing as she prepared for their evening meal. He would come home from an ordinary day of planning sermons and kiss her on the cheek. She would smell like fresh-baked bread and lilac water….

The pain was paralyzing. He'd left part of himself behind that day, and he had taken away enough guilt and remorse to sink him the next time he tried to cross a river.

"The next time it rained," he told Henry, "Anna was terrified. Each river we crossed, I had to hold her on the horse with me and wait out her cries, begging me to turn back." His hand trembled visibly as he opened his palm and raked it down his face. "Abigail has nightmares, and she's only ten. Elisabeth is withdrawn. I don't how I'm going to raise them without my wife, and I have no one to blame but myself."

"You didn't kill your wife, Samuel."

He composed himself to say firmly, "It was my choices that took her away from her safe home." His voice shook with anger, and he steadied it by clearing his throat so he could go on. "I've had a lot of time to think back, and I never asked her if she wanted this. She just went along with the move because it was what I wanted. My dream led her to that river and my selfishness pushed her in. Because of my hasty judgment, she died."

Henry adjusted his weight with a grimace, then asked, "Did you love your wife, Samuel?"

A hoarse declaration burned his throat. "Yes."

"You didn't intentionally put her at risk. Sometimes circumstances are out of our control. You did the best you could. You're answering the call of God on your life, are you not?"

"I thought so. I truly did. But if I am, why did this happen?" Unable to sit, Sam got up, paced to a window and gazed, unseeing. "They dug a hole for her, out there on the prairie. I wrapped her in our wedding quilt. She loved that quilt. And we buried her there, where wagon wheels would roll over and hide the spot."

Henry listened silently.

"We stood there after the others had gone back to their wagons, ready to move on. I was thinking that I hadn't seen it coming. The day had been like any other on the trail. Then Elisabeth looked at me and asked me why God didn't save her mother." He turned to face the reverend. "I didn't have an answer."

"We don't have answers to everything," the other man said.

Sam raised a palm to ask, "But how can I be of use to anyone if I can't help my own daughter? She's thirteen and mature for her age. She needed an answer."

"God doesn't want you to be this hard on your-self," Henry assured him. "You're exhausted and you're grieving. I'm sure First Alliance would understand if you needed some time. You're perfectly welcome to stay here nonetheless."

"No," Sam told him. "I want to work. I need to. I want to plan Sunday sermons and make calls and teach. I need to do it."

If he didn't follow through with his plans, Carrie's death would be for nothing.

Chapter Two

The girls had removed their bonnets, giving Josie an opportunity to admire their neat braids. Elisabeth's hair appeared thick and full; Abigail's was so pale and fine that it shone, while Anna's had darker undertones that complimented her eyes.

"I can't imagine the angels are as pretty as the three of you," she said.

"Father says angels are men," Elisabeth informed her.

"Really? All of them?"

"With names like Michael and Gabriel? Yes, most likely."

"Well, that shoots a hole in all the Christmas pageants, now doesn't it?" Josie replied thoughtfully.

The girls studied her. "What do you mean?" Abigail asked.

"The parts of the angels are always played by

little girls," she explained. "'Behold, I bring you good tidings of great joy' and all."

Elisabeth said nothing. Abigail and Anna exchanged a look.

"Why don't you wash your hands at the pump there," Josie suggested, to move past the uncomfortable moment. "You can help me roll and cut the biscuits."

Anna looked up at her through thick lashes.

"And you may be the cutter. I have a tin can that makes perfect circles."

Anna glanced at Elisabeth, who gave her a barely perceptible nod, before taking the can from Josie and watching while she gathered the ingredients.

The simple task was completed quickly, and the biscuits came from the oven uniform and golden-brown. "Let's call your father, shall we? I'll make a tray for Reverend Martin."

After she'd taken the reverend his food, the Harts gathered informally in the roomy kitchen.

"Will you pray over the meal, sir?" she asked Samuel.

He said a brief blessing for their food, thanking God for His provision.

"Help Mrs. Randolph with the dishes," Samuel said after everyone had eaten.

"Please," she said. "Call me Josie. And I can see to the dishes. Let me show you your rooms so you can get settled."

Anna drew a breath in excitement, and she and Abigail looked at each other.

"There's a room for you, Reverend, and one for the girls to share. When we heard you were coming, I set up another narrow bed. Two can sleep on the larger bed and one on the small one."

He glanced at her, and she noticed creases at the corners of his eyes that he'd earned squinting against the sun. "They've been sleeping cramped together on a feather mattress in the wagon. A real bed will be a pleasure we've all nearly forgotten."

She led them upstairs and showed them the two small rooms with sloping ceilings. Anna immediately spread the top half of her body over the larger bed, spreading her arms wide, her cheek pressed against the quilt. She closed her eyes and sighed.

The exhausting effect of their grueling trip couldn't have been plainer. Samuel exuded strength and purpose, but his stance betrayed weariness. The girls' fatigue was evident, as well, and there was an uncertainty in their expressions that saddened her.

She pushed open the wide windows so a breeze could filter through. "The reverend gets chilled easily, so I keep the parlor warm for him. With the shade trees, it cools off quickly up here, if you open the windows on both sides of the house."

"The rooms are nice," Sam assured her. "Thank you."

"This is the parsonage—and the reverend is unmarried, so he doesn't use these rooms. I simply cleaned and aired them out before your arrival. We weren't sure when you'd be here."

"We'll bring in a few of our belongings. Is there a laundry in town?"

"There is, but I'd be glad to take care of it for you."

"You have no idea what you'd be getting yourself into," he replied. "Our clothing hasn't been properly washed since we left Philadelphia. I'd be more comfortable paying someone."

"The laundry is a small building behind the milliner's shop. You can't miss it."

She excused herself and took care of the dishes and the kitchen, then set out kettles, soap and towels. She made sure Reverend Martin had everything he needed for the evening.

"Thank you, Josie," he said as she prepared to leave.

"I'll come make breakfast for our guests in the morning."

"You spend more time here than you do at your own place," he said with an appreciative smile.

"There's not that much for me to do there," she told him. "I'd rather be useful than sit around and do needlepoint."

He shook his head. "You deserve a family, Josie."

"I guess if I was to have one, God would have given one to me by now," she answered matter-of-factly.

She walked the few blocks toward her home,

enjoying the setting sun and the pleasant summer scent of freshly cut grass from the lot beside Mrs. Wilbur's property.

The Iverson children, along with a couple other neighborhood youngsters, were playing in the yard beside hers as she passed.

"Gretchen! James! Time to come in!" Alice Iverson called from her front steps. She noticed Josie and waved. "How's the reverend?"

"Doing well," she called back. "And the interim preacher arrived today."

"I'll be looking forward to Sunday." Alice ushered her two up the painted porch stairs, and the neighbor children scampered home.

Josie observed the Iversons' movements through the lace curtains of their well-lit dining room windows for a moment before catching herself staring. She turned away to hurry along her own walk and to climb the wooden stairs to the dark and silent two-story house she had once shared with her husband.

After turning her key in the lock, she paused momentarily before pushing open the door.

You deserve a family, Josie. Reverend Martin's words echoed in her mind like footsteps in a barren house. She'd certainly wanted a family her whole life. She'd thought marrying Bram would fulfill her dream, but it wasn't meant to be.

She entered the waiting silence.

After locking the door behind her, she made her

way past the open stairway to the kitchen, where she lit a lamp and put a kettle of water on the stove.

The clock in the parlor chimed the hour and the melodious sound reverberated throughout the rooms. Josie steeped tea and carried a cup with her as she wandered the main floor, ending up in the dining room.

She could probably polish the silver tomorrow. She had invited the ladies to hold their quilting session here later in the week, so she had tablecloths to iron and a luncheon to plan. She stood in the darkened room, sipping from her cup, idly thinking about the menu. Her gaze wandered to the triple windows and the lights on in the house next door.

Her dining room faced the Iversons', and by inching aside the curtain, she could observe the family sitting around the table. Karl Iverson was reading aloud while Alice and the two children sat nearby. Alice held something that looked like an embroidery hoop. Before long, she set down her handiwork, and the four of them bowed their heads.

Josie wished she could hear their prayer. She wondered what their needs were. Perhaps they were all prayers of thanksgiving for their health and family. She let the curtain drop back into place. She had as much to be thankful for as the Iversons. She was healthy. Between inheritances from her father and her late husband, she owned a house, half of a newspaper, and had a generous monthly income. God provided her daily needs plus a whole lot more.

"Thank You, Lord, that You meet all my needs," she said with heartfelt gratitude.

Her thoughts traveled to the Hart family, to those lovely young ladies and the loss and hardships they'd suffered. That day their eyes had spoken of their grief more clearly than any words could have. Reverend Hart possessed a quiet strength. She sensed purpose and dignity in his movements and his words. Something about him kindled suppressed emotions deep inside her. His wife must have been a special person. What a shame those girls wouldn't have their mother as they grew up.

As she rinsed her cup and dried the kettle, she prayed for the Hart family, asking God to comfort them and give them strength and peace.

The house had grown dark, so she lit an oil lamp and carried it to the washroom behind the kitchen, where she bathed and changed into her nightclothes before climbing the stairs to her room.

Since Bram's death, she'd chosen to sleep in a different bedroom than the one she'd shared with him. She'd felt thoroughly alone, and had been compelled to make changes. Margaretta had thrown a conniption when Josie had given all of his belongings to the Lydia Closet at church.

"Bram's barely cold in his grave, and you're erasing him from your life," she'd accused in a hurt tone.

It had been six months after Bram's death, and

Josie had been at a place where she needed to do something to move on. She didn't want to grow old and lonely without making an effort to have a fulfilling life. At the time, Josie had known it would be a waste of breath to share her feelings with Margaretta. "I miss him, too, but someone might as well have use of perfectly good clothing," she'd told her.

"You might afford my son the dignity of preserving his memory."

"I've kept his watch and wedding ring and his Bible," she replied. "I have the entire house by which to remember him."

"No doubt you'll change that now, too." The woman had taken several items of clothing from the stacks and turned her back on Josie.

It was *her* house, Josie had thought all along. She could do with it as she pleased. But she liked it fine just the way it was. She'd selected the furnishings and the decor, so of course it suited her.

No, there was only one thing wrong with the house.... Only one thing that she would change if she had the power. It was painfully, glaringly *empty*.

After Sam sorted through the contents of the wagon to find the things his daughters needed for the night, he brought in the copper tub, heated water and sat with Henry in the parlor while the girls helped each other bathe.

"I'm thinking I need to spend another night with the wagon," he told the other man. "I'm too tired to haul more water for a bath, so I'll get one in town to-morrow."

"You need a solid rest before you push on to Colorado," Henry told him.

Sam agreed with a nod. "I want to hear about your church. About the people. You probably have a list of things you need done. I suppose there are visits to make."

"As one of your first duties, I'd appreciate it if you could call on the Widow Harper. Each spring a few of the men till and plant a garden for her. She's not a sociable woman, doesn't join the other ladies in their activities or come to any gatherings except Sunday-morning service. I think I'm the only one who ever goes to visit her, and it's been a while."

"After my chores in town are accomplished tomorrow, and I've had a bath and haircut, I'll be glad to call on her. Shall I take my daughters with me?"

"You do as you're led," Henry replied. "But if you're concerned they might be underfoot here, don't give it another thought. I won't mind their company. In fact, they might give Josie a break as my companion. She's probably seen enough of this house and my face."

"I'll give them the option," Sam decided. "They have their studies, and I don't want them to have fallen behind in their schooling by the time we reach Colorado."

"They seem like bright young ladies," Henry observed. "I'm sure that won't be a problem."

"Carrie always helped them with their school-work." Sam glanced at the dying embers in the fire-place. "I'm seeing now just how much she did." He looked up. "Have you ever lost someone, Reverend?"

"My Rosemary died in childbirth fifteen years ago," Henry replied. "The baby lived only a few hours. A boy, it was. David."

Fifteen years ago, yet sorrow still tinged his voice when he spoke their names. "I'm sorry for your loss."

"Death doesn't take away the impact they made on our lives or their importance to God." Henry waited until Sam met his eyes. "To be gone from here is to be present in glory. It doesn't feel like it now, but I assure you each day will get a little easier. Each week will add more distance from the pain."

Sam trusted the man's wisdom, but he wished there was a more immediate answer. It was up to him to raise three daughters and make up for the loss of their mother.

"I'll see to emptying the tub now and make sure the girls are settled for the night."

Henry got to his feet.

Sam reached out to steady him. "I'll bank the fire. Go on to your bed now."

"You're going to do fine, Sam. Just fine."

Nothing felt as though that would be the case, but Sam had to believe it anyway. Would he always feel as though he was enduring one difficult day after another? He didn't know what to do about it—except pray the reverend was right.

Chapter Three

Josie loved Mondays. On Mondays she had a fresh slate ahead of her, a palette of days that held endless possibilities. A whole new week in which to accomplish as many things as would fit. And this week was even more exciting because there would be tasks aplenty in looking after the interim preacher and his daughters.

She lit the oven, heated water and set full pitchers and towels outside each bedroom door. While coffee boiled, she fried bacon and mixed batter for flapjacks.

When she checked back, Reverend Martin hadn't picked up his water, so she tapped on the door.

"I'm awake, Josie. C'mon in."

He was lying propped on his pillows. "How are you feeling this morning?" she asked.

"Weak as a baby, and tired of it to be sure."

She placed a towel across his lap, prepared his razor and stirred shaving powder into froth with the brush. She handed him the mirror. "I don't mind shaving you."

She'd performed the task many times when he couldn't bear to move.

"I feel like I've taken a step backward."

"Not at all. Your color is good. That wound is healed, and you're eating well. You're just a little tired."

"Hand me the razor, Josie. Your optimism inspires me to push forward."

She handed him the straightedge. "How would you like your eggs?"

"Any way you turn them out will set just fine with me."

"I'll be back for your water. I could send Reverend Hart in to help you dress this morning."

"You're hereby relieved of that task."

As she reached the kitchen, the back door opened, and the man she'd just spoken of entered the house. His clothing was rumpled and dark whiskers shadowed his jaw. He seemed larger than he had the day before, but his direct gaze had the same disturbing effect on her. She stopped in her tracks and pointed to the ceiling. "You— I left water for you upstairs."

"I slept in the wagon. Today I'll store our belongings and bathe in town. I'll sleep upstairs tonight."

"Forgive my rudeness. I was surprised to see you coming in when I hadn't heard you go out."

"You weren't rude, Mrs. Randolph."

She was embarrassed by her reaction at seeing him and spoke too quickly. "Your whereabouts are none of my business, and you certainly don't have to explain yourself."

"May I take water out to the back porch to wash and shave?"

"Certainly. Of course. I wasn't thinking." She lifted a basin from a nail in the pantry and poured warm water into it. "Let me get soap and a towel for you. After you've had your breakfast, would you mind helping Reverend Martin with his clothing?"

"Won't mind a bit." He nodded, took the things she handed him and headed out.

"You certainly made a fool of yourself, Josie," she said in irritation, then turned back to the stove.

A few minutes later, Abigail and Anna arrived wearing clean dresses. Their freshly washed hair was arranged in loose waves down their backs.

"Well, look at the two of you," Josie said, hands on hips and a smile spread across her face. "Aren't you lovely. I've never seen hair so pretty and shiny in all my days." Her own dark hair was wavy and never tended to stay where she pinned it.

Anna beamed.

"Our mama had pretty hair," Abigail told her.

"If you girls take after her, she must have been beautiful."

"She was," Abigail agreed.

"Are you flattering my sisters?" Elisabeth asked.

Josie turned to the oldest Hart sibling now standing in the doorway. "I complimented them. I see you've worn your hair loose today, too. I like the way it shines."

Elisabeth gave Josie an unreadable glance and took a seat at the table.

Josie prepared a tray and carried it in to where Reverend Martin sat propped in bed, clean-shaven.

"Breakfast smells wonderful," he told her.

She rinsed out his shaving supplies in the clean water left in the pitcher, then carried the supplies from the room.

By then, Samuel had returned with the empty enamel basin.

"Looks like there are quite a few towels to launder today," he said, glancing at the basket in the corner. "I can take them when I go into town."

"That's not necessary. I'll do them," she said. "Monday is my usual laundry day. The girls can help."

Elisabeth's eyes widened. "But we're in a town now. You can send them out, can't you?"

"I don't pay for services I can do myself," Josie answered in surprise. Most preachers earned only a modest income. Reverend Martin kept a strict budget. She glanced at Samuel, now regretting she'd spoken so quickly. Perhaps the Harts had family money. She had no business questioning his expenditures.

"My wife took care of the domestic chores," he

explained. "But I see no reason why my daughters can't learn a bit of self-sufficiency. They'll need the skills sooner than later." He looked at Elisabeth. "This morning while I'm in town, I want the three of you to take directions from Mrs. Randolph. I'm sure she'll be fair about dividing the duties according to your ages and abilities."

Elisabeth's cheeks darkened and she refused to look up at Josie or her father. "Yes, sir."

"Yes, sir," the other two echoed.

"What can I do, Mrs. Randolph?" Anna asked with bright enthusiasm. "I'm a good helper."

"We'll find you a suitable chore," Josie replied, and then gestured for Samuel to take a seat. "Please."

She served the meal she had prepared, and the reverend said grace before they ate.

Elisabeth didn't speak or raise her gaze the entire time.

"Do any girls or boys live by here?" Anna asked.

"There's a family down two houses," Josie replied. "Susanna Maxwell is probably about your age. How old are you?"

"I'm nine," Anna replied proudly. "Can I see your room?"

Josie glanced up. "I don't live here," she explained. "This is the parsonage. I have my own home a few blocks away."

"Oh." Anna set down her fork. "How come you don't eat with your family?"

Elisabeth finally raised her gaze in interest.

Josie touched her napkin to her lips. "I'm a widow."

Anna glanced from her father to Josie with a puzzled expression. "What does *widow* mean?"

"It means my husband died," Josie replied.

Anna seemed to consider that for a minute. "Are you a widow, Papa?"

He held his mouth in a grim line, but he answered, "'Widower' is the term for a man."

"Why?"

"You've asked enough questions for one meal," he said. "Let Mrs. Randolph finish her breakfast."

"Yes, sir." Anna picked up her fork.

Sam explained that he'd be back that afternoon and what their choices were. "When I return, I'll expect you to have decided whether or not you're coming with me when I go calling."

Anna sat on the edge of her chair and beseeched her father with eyes open wide. Her eagerness to say something forced Josie to hold back a laugh.

Samuel set down his cup. "What do you want to ask, Anna?"

Her expression showed her relief. "Who's gonna help me with my letters and numbers?"

Elisabeth and Abigail glanced at each other. Apparently their mother had guided their lessons.

"Until we move on to Colorado and get you settled in a school, Elisabeth will help you."

Anna frowned at her older sister. "She doesn't do it the way Mama did."

"Regardless, she will be your helper over the summer. You will answer to me if she reports you've given her any difficulty. Understood?"

His youngest daughter sat back meekly. "Yes, sir."

He strode from the room.

Elisabeth was an efficient yet silent helper. After the meal was cleaned up, Josie got out the washtubs and heated water. She showed the girls how to make proper suds, scrub the towels and sheets on the washboard, then rinse and run them through the wringer. Anna thought the wringer was great fun, though she needed help to turn it as thick material was fed through.

Elisabeth was the tallest as well as the most precise when it came to hanging the laundry to dry, so she helped Josie while Abigail moved the baskets and handed them clothespins. Elisabeth performed the task capably, spacing the garments just so, using the same number of pins for each neatly stretched sheet.

"You do such a perfect job," Josie told her. "I'd never know you hadn't done this a hundred times before."

Without a word, Elisabeth clamped the last wooden pin to the final pillowcase and wiped her hands on the apron Josie had loaned her. Josie knew the girl would have much preferred her father pay to have the task performed, but that wasn't because she was lazy. Her work had proven that.

At noon Josie sliced ham and cheese for sandwiches. Samuel hadn't returned yet, and she invited the girls to eat in the study with the reverend. From the pleased look on his face, their young guests were just the medicine he needed. Several church members had been faithful visitors and he'd even held a Wednesday-evening study at the house the past few weeks, but months of pain and inactivity had grated on the man who was accustomed to being active and independent.

"Maybe there's a skillful checker player in our midst today," Josie suggested.

Reverend Martin's amused gaze shot to hers. "Your implication has been recorded."

Glad to see him in a cheerful mood, she laughed and a discussion of who would play checkers ensued. "Do you like bread pudding?" she finally asked to deter the subject.

"I love it," Abigail replied. "Mama always made lemon sauce."

"I think I'll make a pan. Would you like to help? I'll go home for my cookbook and find a recipe for lemon sauce."

Abigail's face lit up, but her glance edged to her older sister.

"What about going calling with Father?" Elisabeth asked.

"Papa said we could decide," Abigail replied. "I want to stay here and bake."

"Suit yourself. I'm going with Father."

"Can I come to your house with you?" Anna asked.

"I'd love your company," Josie replied. "It's just a short walk."

"Do you have a dog or a cat?"

Josie shook her head.

"I have Daisy," Reverend Martin said. "Silly cat's been hiding since yesterday."

"You have a cat?" Anna asked.

"I'm guessing she's in that bedroom there. She likes to lie on the window seat in the sun. I wouldn't try to catch her. She might scratch you."

A little while later, Anna enjoyed the yards they passed and asked about the neighbors. Once they reached Josie's, she was fascinated by everything in the house, not touching, but commenting and asking questions.

"Did you live here when you were a little girl?" she asked.

"No," Josie answered. "My father traveled a lot, and my mother and I often stayed at my grandmother's."

"How come you don't have any little girls or boys?"

If Josie couldn't answer that for herself, she certainly didn't know how to explain it to a nine-year-old. "I don't know," she replied. "I just don't."

"Do you want a baby?"

Josie appreciated her innocent candor. She stopped in front of the cupboard where she'd gone to find a cookbook and looked down at Anna. "I wanted a baby very much," she said honestly. "But I have friends and tasks to keep me busy, and I think about the good things I do have, rather than what I don't have."

"That's prob'ly good," Anna said convincingly. She watched Josie select a cookbook. "Was it hard to not think about your mama at first? 'Cause I think about my mama a lot, and it makes me sad."

"I still think about her, but now I remember the time we spent together and the things she taught me. I'm still sad that I don't have her, but missing her doesn't hurt like it used to. It's okay to be sad," she assured the child. "We miss the people we love when they're gone."

Anna nodded solemnly.

Josie had the urge to lean down and hug the child, but Anna barely knew her, and Josie didn't want to overstep. "Now let's find a recipe that sounds like your mama's lemon sauce."

Anna smiled, revealing four new front teeth and a side one missing. She was naively honest, charmingly inquisitive and altogether adorable.

After searching and finding what they wanted, they returned to the reverend's with the cookbook. Elisabeth immediately took Anna aside and spoke to her in soft tones Josie couldn't hear.

Elisabeth hadn't warmed to Josie, and it seemed she wasn't comfortable with the fact that Anna had taken to her. Elisabeth got out a slate and chalk and helped Anna with numbers.

Some time later, Josie and Abigail were planning the evening meal when Samuel rode past the house on horseback. He had obviously bathed and shaved, and his neatly trimmed chestnut hair shone in the sunlight. He wore a new pair of denim trousers, a pale blue shirt and a string tie.

He led the animal into the enclosure and headed toward the house. Josie turned her attention to their list until the pleasing scents of sun-dried clothing and bay rum reached her. Abigail shot across the room to hug him. The holster and revolver still hung at his hip.

He met her gaze, so she asked, "Have you eaten?"

"Haven't had time to think about food, truthfully."

"I'll make you something you can take along."

"That's kind of you. Who's coming with me?"

"Elisabeth," Abigail answered. "I'm going to help Mrs. Randolph make bread pudding. We have a recipe for lemon sauce."

"That's fine." Samuel nodded. "And you'll work on your studies. Run and fetch Elisabeth for me, please. Where's Anna?"

"She found Reverend Martin's cat," Abigail answered on her way toward the hall. "Right now she's watching it sun itself."

One corner of his mouth inched up, and Josie found herself intrigued by the possibility of a smile on his clean-shaven face.

He looked back and found her gaze on him. "Would you prefer I take Anna along, since Elisabeth won't be here to look after her?"

"Anna's no trouble," she replied. "If she wants to stay, I'll keep an eye on her."

"Thank you, Mrs. Randolph."

"Would you mind calling me Josie? When I hear you say Mrs. Randolph I look for my mother-in-law—a fine woman of God," she clarified quickly.

He raised his chin in half a nod.

She sliced bread and made a sandwich that she wrapped and handed to him. "There's a basket of apples just inside the pantry if you'd like to take a couple. You and Elisabeth might get hungry before you return."

He accepted the sandwich and met her gaze. His eyes were the color of glistening sap on a maple tree. The degree of sadness and disillusionment she read in their depths never failed to touch her. She wished she could do something that would remove that look.

"Your kindness is what my daughters need right now, Josie." They were alone in the kitchen, yet he spoke softly as though he didn't want to be over-heard. "They've been through a lot." He paused and his throat worked.

His loss was so recent, his pain so fresh. He'd obviously loved his wife very much. Josie didn't presume to know how the man felt, and she knew words wouldn't help right now. She understood and respected his grief.

She found her voice. "They're lovely children, Reverend."

"Every time I look at them, I see how fragile they are. How young and…" Samuel glanced away. "And vulnerable. They're hurting." He drew his gaze back to hers. "Elisabeth is handling it her own way, and I know she's difficult. But…well, thank you for understanding."

"I don't believe in coincidence."

Samuel's eyes showed a spark of interest. "What do you mean?"

Chapter Four

"You're here for a reason," Josie answered. "I'm open to whatever God has planned."

He didn't say anything, but he swallowed hard and nodded.

Elisabeth entered the room, followed by Abigail. Elisabeth paused and glanced from her father to Josie. "I'm going with you." She raised her hem, revealing a pair of trousers under her skirt.

"I figured as much, so I saddled the other horse. Let's grab a couple of apples and head out."

Josie and Abigail followed them onto the back steps and watched as father and daughter mounted their horses.

Abigail waved until they were out of sight. Josie was beginning to wonder if the girl was sorry she hadn't gone along, until Abigail turned wide, eager eyes to her. "Can we start now?"

Josie agreed with a smile and they went back in. Buttering a baking dish, she asked, "Do you like to ride?"

She shook her head. "Not so much. Do you?" Abigail studied all the ingredients on the table. "What should I do?"

"Tear this bread into little pieces and drop them in the pan," Josie said before answering her other question. "I think I'd like to. I haven't been on a horse since I was small, and my uncle took me."

Abigail picked up the bread. "We only took carriages in Philadelphia. I never rode, till Papa told us we were moving to Colorado. He said we needed to learn, and he taught us."

Josie cracked eggs into a bowl and whipped them with a fork. "I've never been to a city as big as Philadelphia. I've lived here most of my life. What were your favorite things to do back home?"

"I liked school." Abigail layered the bottom of the pan with bits of torn bread. "And parades. And when school was out we took tea in the afternoon, so we still got to see our friends when their mothers brought them or we went to their houses. May I put in the cinnamon?"

"Two teaspoonfuls. That sounds like fun." Josie enjoyed how she and Abigail often held two conversations at once.

"Oh, it was. My Mama has a china tea set with violets painted on the pot and the cups." She paused on the last chunk of bread. "I wonder where it is."

"Your father put your things in storage. I'm sure he was careful to store the tea set where it would be safe."

Abigail dropped in the last piece of bread, measured the cinnamon and then brushed her hands together with a flourish. "Now what?"

"Now we whip the egg mixture, pour it over the top and bake it."

"Was this in the recipe book, too?"

"Actually, no. I just remember how, from seeing my mother do it."

"Maybe we better write it down so I can remember when we get to Colorado. I might wanna make it for my papa."

Josie studied Abigail's serious blue eyes. The afternoon sun streaming through the window caught her pale hair and made it glisten. The girl's foresight touched her. She'd lost her mother, and she needed to cling to familiar things. She needed to feel safe. "That's a very good idea. In fact, I'll make you a little book of all the recipes we use together."

Her expressive face brightened. "You will?"

Josie nodded. Just then, Anna called them to come observe the cat batting at a fly on the windowsill. The child was fascinated by the feline's swift movements, and then grimaced when it caught the insect and ate it. Josie hid her amusement. "I have an idea."

"What is it?" Anna asked.

"I have a tea set. Why don't you and Abigail come home with me for an hour or so, and we'll have tea."

Anna scrambled to her feet. "Do you got any lemon cakes or raisin scones?"

"I don't, but I have some sugar cookies. Those will do, won't they?"

Anna's delighted smile was all the answer required.

The afternoon passed more quickly than any Josie could remember. After they'd had tea and cleaned up, then taken the sheets from the line and folded them, the girls got comfortable on their bed and read while Josie made up the reverend's bed with fresh sheets and put away the towels.

She waited supper until Samuel and Elisabeth arrived. Josie ate in the kitchen with the girls, while Samuel kept Henry company, so they could talk about the calls he'd made. The bread pudding was well received, and Reverend Martin even asked for seconds. She refused offers of help to wash the dishes, and the girls went up to their room to study.

Later, she made coffee and carried a tray to the men and served them.

"Sit with us," Reverend Martin invited. "Unless you have to be going."

She hesitated only momentarily. Evenings were dreadfully long at her house. She jumped at the chance to avoid another one. "I'll get a cup."

Samuel stood until she had poured her coffee and taken a seat. "Your daughters are delightful company," she told him. "I think even Daisy is warming to Anna."

Henry explained how Anna and the feline had held a staring match most of the afternoon. He raised one eyebrow. "Sam said the Widow Harper seemed a trifle standoffish."

Josie knew the woman. Mrs. Harper had been a widow for as long as Josie could remember, though others in town recalled a husband.

"And it seems she's added a chicken to her pets since I was there last," he told her.

"There was a sheep in a pen right beside the front door," Sam said.

"I knew about the lamb," Josie said. "I guess it grew up and was too big for the parlor."

"She's not too keen on people," Henry understated. "Prefers her critters."

"She didn't care much for our visit," Samuel told them. "Feeling was mutual, actually. Elisabeth sat on a footstool with her gaze riveted on that chicken, like it was going to fly up and peck her eyes out at any minute."

Josie fought back a laugh by pursing her lips. Finally, she managed to say, "I would probably have done the same."

Reverend Martin laughed then, a chuckle that started slow and built, until he held his sore ribs and grimaced.

Samuel's cheek creased becomingly in a grin that gradually spread across his face.

Why his crooked smile was of special interest, she couldn't have said, but the sight warmed and lifted Josie's heart.

His laugh, once it erupted, was a deep, resonating sound that Josie felt through the floorboards. She knew instinctively that laughing was something he hadn't done for a long time. She joined their merriment with a burst of laughter.

A shriek came from upstairs, effectively silencing their good humor. The sound came again, followed by a thump on the floor above.

Samuel shot from his chair and Josie followed close behind. He took the stairs two at a time while she gathered her hem and kept a slower pace.

The lamp on the hallway wall led them to the girls' bedroom, and Samuel darted in. Josie found the oil lamp on the bureau and lit it.

She couldn't identify the sobbing, but Abigail's father went unerringly to the larger bed, where the covers were strewn onto the floor and Abigail sat with her arms over her head, white-clad elbows pointed toward the ceiling.

Elisabeth sat up from the narrow bed where she slept alone and blinked sleepily at them.

Anna was on her knees on the mattress beside Abigail, reaching out to stroke her sister's mussed hair.

"It was Mama," Abigail choked out, tears glistening on her cheeks. "Mama was in the water."

Behind her, Anna burst into tears.

Samuel lifted Abigail and she wrapped her arms and legs around his waist and clung to him. He splayed one hand across her back and smoothed her hair with the other, making comforting shushing sounds.

Anna's sobs broke Josie's heart, and the sight of Sam holding Abigail so tenderly stirred feelings from her childhood, reminded her she'd never been held and comforted by her father. She couldn't just stand by and do nothing, so she went to the side of the bed and knelt to touch Anna's arm.

Anna immediately lunged toward her, her weight taking Josie by surprise and nearly toppling her. She regained her balance and sat on the edge of the bed, where Anna nestled right into her lap and tucked her head under her chin. The sweet scent of her hair and her trembling limbs incited all of Josie's nurturing instincts. The girls' heartbreaking sobs brought a lump to her throat and moisture to her eyes. She held Anna securely, rubbing her back and rocking without conscious thought. After a few minutes, Anna's sobs dwindled.

Josie recalled her poignant words about her mother. Her gaze touched on a rag doll lying on the floor, then moved to the narrow bed where Elisabeth had lain back down and was staring at her. Josie stroked Anna's back and gave Elisabeth an encouraging smile. The girl pulled the sheet up around her shoulders and rolled to face the other way.

"It was just a dream, Ab," Samuel said to his daughter. "Just a dream."

"But it was real." Her voice trembled as she explained. "It was just like the day Mama died. I could hear the water…."

At those words, Anna trembled again in Josie's arms. *Oh, Lord, please comfort these children.*

"And I could see her."

"I know," Samuel said. "I know." He lowered her to the bed and perched beside her on the edge opposite where Josie sat holding Anna. In the lantern light, his face was etched with shared suffering. He gathered the bedding and covered Abigail with the sheet. "Dreams do seem very real."

Abigail snuggled into the bedding.

"Remember the psalm we found?" Samuel asked her.

She nodded. "Will you say it, Papa?"

"'When thou liest down, thou shalt not be afraid; yea thou shalt lie down, and thy sleep shall be sweet.'" His voice and those inspired words sent a shiver up Josie's spine.

Sam closed his eyes. "Merciful Lord, give Abigail and Anna and Elisabeth sweet sleep this night."

"Yes, Lord," Abigail said and closed her eyes.

"Yes, Lord," Josie said under her breath.

The remaining tension drained from Anna's frame and she relaxed.

Josie's chest ached with compassion for this man and his daughters. She admired his love for them, his dedication to their well-being, and was moved by his trust in God to comfort them. They had no idea how blessed they were to have a father who was present in their lives.

Samuel opened his eyes and nodded at Josie. She urged Anna from her lap, and the child slid under the covers to snuggle beside her sister.

"Good night, Mrs. Randolph," Anna whispered. "Thanks for the hugs."

She wanted to cry herself, but instead she gave the child a reassuring smile. "Good night, Anna."

Josie turned out the lamp and followed Samuel into the hallway, where he pulled the door closed and stood in the golden light of the wall lantern. When he met her eyes, she read his anguish.

"I never know what to say," he told her.

"You said exactly the right things," she assured him. "And you're there for them, that's what's important. When they need you, you're there."

"It doesn't seem like enough."

"We're never enough in our own ability," she assured him. "When we acknowledge that is when God works through us. And He worked through you in there."

He turned his face aside, and his voice was thick when he said, "Thank you."

She gathered her hem and moved toward the stairs.

Sam watched her leave, his thoughts a little less confusing than they'd been for some time. He recalled what she'd said about not believing in co-incidence. It was no accident that his family was staying in this house. He'd been desperate, thinking he was unable to help his daughters. He'd prayed for guidance, for wisdom, for the weight of the burden to be lifted.

And now, for the first time in months, Sam didn't feel quite so alone.

Josie took the hot iron from the stove and pressed the wrinkles from a pair of plain white pillowcases. The previous evening had been on her mind all morning. A girl as young and sweet as Abigail shouldn't have nightmares. Her terror had stricken fear into Anna, as well. But their anguish was understandable, considering all they'd gone through.

While it was difficult to observe the younger girls' misery, Elisabeth's detachment from the episode was what bothered Josie the most. Elisabeth had watched her sisters until meeting Josie's gaze, and then she'd turned away—as though unwilling to admit any part in it or to show her feelings. Josie folded the pillowcases and glanced over at Abigail, who was sitting at the table reading a book. Anna was probably cat-watching, and unless her father was present, Elisabeth spent most of her time upstairs.

"What are you reading?" Josie asked.

The girl marked her place with an index finger and looked up. "It's a story about a boy growing up on a farm. Farms sound like great fun. Have you ever lived on one?"

"No, but I've visited quite a few. We're in the middle of farm country."

"Maybe we could go see."

"A lot of the members of our congregation are farmers. If you went along with your father when he makes his calls, you'd get to see where they live."

"Really?" Abigail looked excited for a moment, but then her expression changed. "Elisabeth joins Papa when he goes calling. Unless there's school, of course. Do you suppose she saw a farm yesterday?"

Was Abigail feeling unwelcome? "She may have."

Abigail slid a delicate, tatted marker in the shape of a cross between the pages and closed her book. "I'm gonna go ask her." She scampered up the stairs.

A knock sounded on the back door, and Josie set the iron on the stove to see who was calling. Grace Hulbert stood holding what appeared to be a pie covered with a dish towel.

"Come in," Josie greeted her. "The reverend's in the parlor."

"I brought an apple pie for the traveling preacher and his family," Grace told her, peeling back the fabric to reveal a golden-brown crust with a perfectly crimped edge. "Is he here? The preacher man?"

"No, he's out."

"Is it true he's a widower?"

"Sadly so. His wife drowned." Josie took the pie and set it inside the tin-fronted safe.

"They say he wears a holster and a gun about town. Is it so?"

Josie wondered where that question had come from. "I'm certain everyone on their wagon train needed a gun to protect themselves—and to hunt. Is that so unusual?"

"It's unusual for a man of the cloth. Has he shot anyone?"

"I have no idea, Grace. What kind of question is that?"

Grace pinched off her white gloves one finger at a time. "He's the latest bachelor in town, so of course there's speculation."

"Bachelor?" Josie's temperature rose a degree. Grace was a married woman, but she had a daughter who'd been on the shelf since her fiancé ran off six months ago. Josie leveled her gaze on the woman. "Would you like to visit with Reverend Martin? He's in the parlor."

"Oh, no." She had one glove off and stopped removing the other. "I have to run. I just wanted to leave the pie."

"I'll let Reverend Martin know you were here."

Grace headed for the door, but Anna appeared just then. "May I help with the ironing?"

"Is this one of the traveling preacher's daughters?" Grace asked, turning back.

"This is Anna. Anna, Mrs. Hulbert."

"How do you do, Mrs. Hulbert," she said shyly.

"I do quite well, thank you, Anna. It's a pleasure to meet you. You're sure a pretty little thing. Do you take after your father?"

Anna moved to stand beside Josie and seemed disinclined to respond.

"You can sprinkle the sheets to dampen them while I see Mrs. Hulbert out," Josie told her. "Then we'll figure out what to fix for lunch."

Grace didn't give her a chance to move to the door. "I'll be going."

She let herself out and the door clicked shut. Josie stared at it for a moment, absorbing that odd exchange. The women of Durham were looking upon Samuel Hart as a *bachelor?* She tried to shake off the disgust that knowledge made her feel.

Anna was gazing up at her with a curious wrinkle in her brow. "Do I take after my Papa?"

Josie took a sheet from the basket. "Of the three of you, your eyes are most like his. Yours lend themselves to green sometimes, though. Like today, in that pretty green calico dress."

Anna looked down and wrinkled her freckled nose. "This old thing was Abby's."

"You're fortunate to have sisters who wore such nice clothing and took good care of it."

The child cocked her head. "Papa says some little girls don't have nice dresses at all, and they would love to have hand-me-downs."

"Your papa's right."

"He says it's foolish to buy new dresses, when we already have perfectly good ones that fit me soon enough."

Josie understood the practicality of reusing their

clothing, but she also knew the pleasure of having a new dress. "Surely you've had a new dress."

"I get one for my birthday every year. And one when school starts. But people saw Abigail wear all these other ones."

"You won't have that problem now, will you?" she asked. "You're meeting all new people, and they won't know someone wore that dress before you."

Anna smiled her charming missing-tooth smile and all was well for the rest of the afternoon.

That evening, Josie prepared their meals and served the reverend and his houseguest in the study. Samuel thanked her, and she met his eyes. Grace Hulbert's brash curiosity came to mind immediately. If Grace could see the pain that Josie read in his eyes, she wouldn't be thinking of him as though he were a prize horse up for sale to the highest bidder.

Josie ate in the kitchen with the girls. They were just finishing when Sam carried in his and the reverend's dishes. "You're an excellent cook, Mrs. Randolph."

She looked over at him with a raised brow.

"I mean Josie. Thank you."

"You're welcome. Mrs. Hulbert brought pie for your family."

He set down the plates. "That was kind. Why don't we have it later this evening? Girls, I'd like you to help Mrs. Randolph with the dishes."

"Shouldn't we work on our studies?" Elisabeth asked.

"Tomorrow's Sunday. Make sure your clothing is ready, and then, after our family time, you may enjoy the evening any way you like."

Elisabeth looked at Josie. "Our Sunday dresses need to be pressed."

"I'll get out the irons for you," Josie answered.

"I don't know how to iron," Elisabeth replied.

"It's not difficult. I'll show you how."

"I know how to sprinkle," Abigail added cheerfully.

Elisabeth cast her father a beseeching look.

"Thank you," he said to Josie. "Elisabeth is a quick learner. And she will help with her sisters' dresses, as well."

Elisabeth's shoulders drooped. "Yes, sir."

"Papa?" Abigail asked. "When you go calling at a farm, can I come with you? Mrs. Randolph said the parishioners are mostly farmers, an' I want to see their animals."

"Of course you may come, Abby."

"Will Elisabeth come that day, too?"

He blinked, but didn't pause in replying, "We'll talk about it. After your dresses are pressed, I'd like the three of you to get your wraps and come for a walk with me."

"At night?" Anna asked.

"Night is when you can see God's heavens most clearly," he replied.

"Yes, sir," they replied one at a time.

Josie kept the stove hot and set two irons on top.

Abigail sprinkled their dresses and, using Elisabeth's dress, Josie showed them how to press the collars and sleeves first, then the bodice and lastly the skirts. Elisabeth did an adequate job on her sisters' clothing, and they carried their dresses upstairs and hung them.

The girls came down with capes and bonnets, and the Hart family swept out of doors, leaving the house silent.

Sam held Anna's delicate hand in his, feeling the weighty responsibility of protecting these daughters he loved so well. He'd never felt so inadequate or so incomplete, and he didn't like it. He'd been very careful laying plans for safety and finances, and so far he'd seen most of his puny plans thrown back in his face.

So far, Josie had been the best thing that had happened to them since they'd left home. He didn't want to take advantage of her kindness or overload her with their additional care. Her kindness and selfless generosity was like a healing balm to his conscience, and he hoped her attention would be healing for his daughters, as well.

"While we are guests in the parsonage, I want the three of you to help as much as you can. Mrs. Randolph already cares for Reverend Martin's needs, and we are an added burden. Your mother and I didn't prepare you for this life. I know that. She took care of you, and things were easy in Philadelphia. I told you it would be an adventure coming west, but I didn't tell you about all the difficulties. On top of everything else, your mother's absence is an exceptional hardship."

"We'll help, Father," Elisabeth assured him.

"We'll do everything we're asked, and make our beds and wash dishes," Abigail agreed.

"I like Mrs. Randolph," Anna said. "She's real nice, and she smells good."

"Mrs. Randolph is a very kind lady," Sam agreed. He appreciated the woman's warm concern and easy affection for his children. Surely the Lord had brought her and his daughters together to ease their way through this life transition.

He considered the possibility that Anna—and perhaps even Abigail—would come to lean on her and then have another heartbreak when they moved on. It could likely happen in the weeks that they would be here.

But an unexplainable assurance convinced him that her attention and warmth were exactly what the girls—all three of them—needed right now. He didn't doubt that God could use Josie to help their family, if she was willing. And she certainly seemed willing.

"I'm going to take care of you," he said with heartfelt conviction. And he would. He was all they had now, and he was going to do everything he could to protect them and see that they had a good life.

Chapter Five

After turning down the reverend's bed, Josie brought him a slice of pie and a cup of coffee. "I guess I'll be going."

"Take your leave if you have something to do, Josie. I'll be fine. Otherwise, sit and have coffee with me."

She didn't need to be asked twice. Josie got herself a cup and settled on a comfortable chair.

"They fill this place with life," Reverend Martin commented, referring to his guests.

Her smile came readily. "That they do."

"That's how I've felt about your being here these last couple of months," he said. "I'd forgotten how nice it is to hear someone in the other room and have conversation at meal time. I've enjoyed having a companion."

"It's been no hardship. I was glad to do it."

"I know you were." He sipped coffee, then set down his cup. "I've been thinking about something, and I just can't get the idea out of my head."

She studied him and waited. He'd lost weight, and the pain had etched a few lines beside his mouth that hadn't been there before. His hair was still dark and his eyes were as kind as ever.

"Maybe this is a poor time to bring this up, but I have to say it. I've enjoyed our time together, Josie. I know taking on another house and caring for me has been a chore for you, but you've never complained. In fact, in most ways, it seems we've gotten along well, even though I'm not at my finest. You've seen the worst of me, and you haven't lit out."

She laughed easily. "You don't have to thank me. Your worst is easily some people's best."

"Well. You've seen who I am. And I've gotten to know you pretty well, too, I think. What I'm trying to say is that…maybe we had this time for a reason."

She studied him curiously.

"I'm not at my best, obviously. But I'm getting there, slowly but surely. I won't be tied down forever. In a few more weeks I'll be back to normal. The Harts will move on, and life will resume as it once was."

Though she didn't want to think of that day, she nodded her agreement. "Yes."

"But we don't have to go back to the way it was. You're a good friend, Josie. I can be a good companion as soon as I can get around. We've both been married before and lost someone, and we can respect that former part of our lives. I wouldn't expect to replace Bram, because I'm not him. But we don't have to be lonely."

Henry Martin's words slowly permeated her thinking, and Josie tried to put them in order in her head. Enjoyable time together. Companionship. Not being lonely. She studied the dancing flames for a moment before casting an incredulous gaze on him. "Are you suggesting what I think you're suggesting?"

"I'm not doing a proper job of it, am I?" He frowned. "When I'm able, I'll get down on one knee—"

"That's not necessary."

"But yes, I'm asking you to marry me. I'm extremely fond of you, Josie. Marry me and come live here with me. Or I'd live in your home if you preferred. As long as we kept each other company…"

Marry him and move him into her house? An image of Margaretta in a disapproving tirade loomed in Josie's mind, and she had to blink away the picture. She gathered her tumbling thoughts. "Reverend—"

"Henry. I'm a few years older than you are, of course, but not that many. Years don't really mean anything."

"I hadn't even thought of that."

"What did you think of?"

"Well…nothing yet. I haven't had time to think."

"Of course you haven't. I just dropped it on you. There's no hurry."

She nodded and rose to stand. She needed to go home.

"Josie."

She looked at him.

He extended a hand.

She took it and held it.

"Think it over," he said softly. "You've been alone for several years. I've been alone for fifteen. We could keep each other company for the rest of our lives and, God willing, that will be a good, long time."

She nodded. "I will. I'll think it over." She released his hand. "Good night. I'll come fix breakfast before church in the morning."

He nodded. "Thank you."

She turned back once to look at him, her thoughts a jumble in her mind. Josie stepped out into the night and walked toward home. It was dark now, and as she passed the Iversons', she could see the family gathered in the parlor. Alice had never bothered closing shades or drapes. Josie's neighbor had nothing to hide.

Marry the reverend? Her thoughts tumbled one over the other.

Alice and Reggie had been married shortly after Josie had married Bram and come to live here. From her next-door vantage point and during occasional visits over the hedge, Josie had witnessed the arrival of Alice's children, seen guests coming and going for family holidays and birthdays and admired the natural flow of their lives. From her viewpoint, it was all quite imposing and foreign.

She'd pretty much resigned herself to being alone, and had found activities to keep her busy. She'd taken on volunteer work to make herself feel useful.

Josie unlocked her door and stepped into the echoing silence of her house. Closing her eyes, she leaned back against the door. No voices here. Nothing of importance for which to set aside chores. No scuffed floors or tangle of sweaters and shoes. No reason not to stay up reading half the night.

Josie didn't feel like stoking and lighting the stove just for a single cup of tea, so the coffee she'd shared with the reverend would suffice.

The reverend. She struggled to think of him as *Henry.* Using his first name seemed disrespectful. Definitely awkward.

If she married him, her motivation wouldn't be for a grand love. She would be striving for companionship. He'd said it as plainly as that, although he had mentioned he'd grown fond of her. Ignoring for a moment the reaction of her mother-in-law, she let herself imagine him living here with her. She would have someone to share her meals and someone to share the fire of an evening. Guests would drop by. Josie pictured ushering them in and pouring them tea and serving cookies and slices of pie.

An uncertain smile curved her lips upward.

Perhaps the reverend would continue to hold his Wednesday-evening Bible studies. She could make an adequate place for the participants in the drawing room.

After lighting the lamp in her room, she undressed and used tepid water to wash before slipping on her nightclothes. It was a warm evening, so Josie opened her bedroom window, welcoming the breeze. She was wide-awake.

Running her fingers over the spines of the books on her bureau, she selected one and made herself comfortable in her padded rocking chair.

She had read the first page at least half a dozen times, without remembering the words, before she closed the book and turned down the wick so the room was thrust into darkness.

Padding to the window, she held aside the curtain and studied the sky. *Lord, help me know the right thing to do,* she prayed. The words to a hymn came to mind, and she sang them softly. *Leave to thy God to order and provide; in every change He faithful will remain.*

Her stomach felt funny when she thought of marrying Reverend Martin. Was that a good sign or a bad one? He hadn't been in a rush for her answer, and she was relieved about that.

He was a kind man. Attentive. He engaged her in conversation and was interested in her thoughts and opinions. Perhaps it was irreverent to compare him to her late husband, but she couldn't help the thoughts. Bram had cared more that she was listening to his instructions and plans than for what she had to say. She'd never felt that she was a priority in his life. Well, in all truth, she hadn't been.

But she didn't need all that much attention. Memories of her father surfaced, reminding her of a childhood spent feeling unimportant. He'd traveled during all of her growing-up years, stopping home only briefly every few months, and even at those times he'd caught up on business, entertained friends, scarcely paying her a moment's notice before he was gone again.

And then her marriage expectations had been too high. She'd believed a wife held value and significance, but though Bram was present, he'd closed her out. Especially after she hadn't given him children. A wife who was unable to give a man children held even less value, apparently.

Henry Martin didn't need or want children. He wanted companionship. He enjoyed her company. And she considered him a teacher and a friend. Could a marriage like that be satisfying? She suspected it could. Having someone who listened and valued her presence would be a far cry better than her current situation. Better than nothing and no one. The thought lifted her spirits. Already, the decision didn't seem all that difficult.

Sam appreciated the tidy little room Josie had assigned him. He woke up a couple of times the first night, thinking he was still sleeping under the wagon. Then the dark and quiet room came into focus, and he remembered where he was.

He'd stayed up late, going over his notes, reading his Bible and praying. He asked God to help him fix his mind on heavenly things and plant his feet on the promises. He didn't doubt God's love or faithfulness. If for a moment he felt that he couldn't preach with heartfelt conviction, he would have resigned then and there. But it wasn't God he doubted; it was himself.

He had to find a way to help his daughters. If he couldn't lead his own sheep, how could he hope to counsel and guide an entire flock? The message he prepared was from First Corinthians, one of his favorite chapters, and he wanted to share what those verses about love meant to him.

On Sunday morning the little church filled to capacity with townspeople and farm families eager to shake his hand and introduce themselves. They'd been without a normal service for months, and this was an occasion to worship and socialize. He took particular comfort in reminding the people of Durham that God is love, and that He's not keeping track of sins or mistakes.

One of the ladies had organized a simple meal afterward, with sliced meat and cheese for sandwiches and a selection of pies and cakes. Sam barely glimpsed the food before members of the congregation sought him out and greeted him, one or two at a time.

He enjoyed meeting all of them, from the youngest to the oldest. After introducing his girls several times, he quietly suggested they go make their own plates and eat without him. Elisabeth obediently took Anna's hand and led both of her sisters toward the tables.

Glancing away from Mrs. Swanson, who prattled on about her cousin who was coming to visit soon, Sam spotted Josie making a sandwich. She cut a slice of pie and carried the plate toward the parsonage. Reverend Martin was a blessed man to have her looking out for him. Out of nowhere came the question of why she'd never remarried, why no man had snapped her up.

She would make a fine wife. A good companion.

"Max Wilbur," a lanky fellow with a yellowed mustache said by way of introduction. "Fine sermon this mornin'. So you're headed for Colorado."

Sam shook the man's hand. "In a few weeks, yes. I've been assigned a church there."

"Ever seen the Rockies?"

"I have not."

"Wild, beautiful country," Max said, and told Sam about his early prospecting days.

"We're so pleased you're here," a stout, dark-haired woman said, coming up beside Max. She held out a gloved hand. "Grace Hulbert, and this is my daughter, Becka."

In turn, Sam took both the hands offered.

"Becka plays the piano," Grace told him. "And she has a very pleasant singing voice."

The young woman was tall and slender, with a long neck and cinnamon-colored red hair. Without meeting Sam's eyes, she smiled bashfully and blushed a color that nearly matched her hair.

"She's a good seamstress and knows how to put up vegetables and preserves. She made the peach pie. Make sure you try a slice."

"She must be your right hand," Sam said. His stomach growled, and he inched toward the food table. Ladies smiled and served him. Finally holding a full plate, he stabbed a slice of pickled beet and raised his fork.

"There you are, Reverend!"

He turned to greet yet another parishioner.

After taking Reverend Martin his meal, Josie returned to spot a throng of women surrounding Samuel Hart. He held a full plate and nodded with seeming interest as they chattered and boasted of their daughters.

His own three daughters were perched on a bench in the shade of the church, where they'd been enjoying their meal. She prepared herself a plate and joined them. "Looks like everyone wants to talk to your father."

Munching a cookie, Anna swung feet clad in freshly polished black leather shoes. She spared a grin for Josie.

"We're going to a farm later today," Abigail told her.

"Won't that be an adventure?" Josie replied and bit into her chicken leg.

"Want to come?" Abigail asked.

"Mrs. Randolph wasn't invited," Elisabeth pointed out.

"I just did so invite her," Abigail argued.

"By *Father*," the older girl clarified.

"Oh. Well, he won't care," Abigail said.

"I don't need to come along," Josie told them. "But thanks for thinking of me."

The crowd around their father still hadn't thinned.

"I want a lamb," Anna announced.

"We can't have an animal," Elisabeth told her. "We don't even have a home yet. And how would we get it all the way from here to Colorado?"

"It could ride with me."

"Lambs get big and they smell," Elisabeth pointed out. "Father and I saw one at a lady's house, and it was shaggy and dirty."

"My lamb wouldn't smell. I'd give it baffs."

Elisabeth rolled her eyes, picked up her bread and bit into it.

It wasn't long before Josie realized that every mother of a marriage-aged daughter had approached Samuel, and the interruptions were preventing him from eating.

"Do any of you want a slice of pie?" she asked.

"I do," Anna piped up. "Apple, please!"

"I'll be right back." Josie moseyed toward the pie

table and placed a slice of pie on a small plate. She interrupted Nettie Boardman as she talked to Samuel about her daughter, the new schoolteacher. "Excuse me, Reverend, but Anna asked for this."

She pushed the plate into Samuel's other hand and pointed toward his daughters.

He blinked in puzzlement, but then his eyes revealed dawning appreciation of her rescue mission. "Thanks, Mrs. Randolph." He turned to Nettie. "Excuse me, ma'am. It's been a pleasure."

Nettie and Josie watched him join his daughters.

"He speaks with such fervor," Nettie said. "His sermon was positively inspired, wasn't it? How long do you suppose he'll be here?"

"Just until Reverend Martin is on his feet again."

"Maybe he'll decide to stay. Maybe he'll meet someone…you know."

Josie picked up on the woman's interest and tried not to show her irritation. "The man just lost his wife. He's determined to go on to his destination."

"Well, plans change." Nettie waved a hand dismissively and turned away.

Josie returned to the Harts, where Sam had seated himself on the grass and dug into his food. He glanced up as she resumed her seat beside Anna. "Thanks."

"You were looking a mite faint there. I thought you needed nourishment."

He grinned. "And air."

Josie returned his smile.

Elisabeth glanced from her father to Josie and back again.

"I think I've met nearly everyone," he said.

She wanted to add "and their daughters," but said, "So it would seem."

Gretchen Iverson ran over to where they sat. "Hello, Mrs. Randolph."

Josie made introductions. "Anna asked me about nearby children. I think you're right between Anna and Abigail's ages."

"Wanna come play?" Gretchen asked.

Anna jumped right up, and Abigail joined her more slowly. After a brief conversation, they ran toward a gathering of young females jumping rope.

Elisabeth watched them go and then turned her gaze on her father.

"This is what they need," he said. "It's good for them to resume normal activities and be with other children."

Josie wondered if being around people and using his gifts was something he needed, as well. She'd appreciated his heartfelt words that morning. He had a resonating voice and a sincerity that one couldn't help but recognize. God's wisdom was evident in calling this man to the ministry.

At the sound of stiff skirts swishing through the grass, they turned their attention to Margaretta's approach.

Chapter Six

She wore a black gabardine dress and a pinched expression.

"Reverend Hart, this is my mother-in-law, Margaretta Randolph."

Sam stood and brushed crumbs from his trousers. "Mrs. Randolph. It's a pleasure to meet you."

"Likewise," she replied without much fervor.

"This is Sam's oldest daughter, Elisabeth," Josie added.

The woman raised her eyebrows at the introduction, but barely nodded. "Are you ready to visit my son?"

"I'll walk back there with you." Josie spoke to Sam then. "We visit the cemetery on Sunday afternoons."

Sam nodded politely, and she followed Margaretta. Seeing the woman reminded her of the decision she had to make regarding Reverend Martin's proposal.

As strongly as the woman felt about giving away Bram's clothing and visiting his grave, Josie sensed that an announcement of a new marriage wouldn't be received well. She couldn't let disapproval make up her mind for her, but she wished she had someone with whom to discuss the possibilities.

They entered the well-tended cemetery through the white picket gate in the fence and crossed the lush cropped grass, picking their way around small headstones.

Margaretta stopped at Bram's grave and pulled her hankie from her pocket. Cue the tears, Josie thought.

"Margaretta, I'd like to talk to you."

The woman sniffled. How could she still call up tears after all this time? "Bram left you plenty of money," she said.

Josie stiffened with hurt. "So did my father. It's not about money."

"What do you want?"

"When have I ever asked you for anything? You're the closest thing I have to family. I thought we could talk." She glanced away. The afternoon was stretching out clear and fair. Back by the church, people were packing up and heading home. "I'm still a young woman," she began. "I'm lonely."

"We all have our crosses to bear," Margaretta replied.

Josie lowered her attention to study the familiar words on the headstone. *Beloved son and husband.* Even in death, her mother-in-law came before her. Josie's gaze drifted beyond the cemetery to the fluffy white clouds in the sky and the tops of the leafy oak trees along the stream. The sounds of children's laughter rang out.

"Don't do anything to embarrass me in this town."

Margaretta spoke the words like a warning, effectively pointing out Josie's foolishness in thinking the woman would suddenly feel a measure of compassion toward her son's widow. Why was Margaretta compelled to issue such an admonition? What did she imagine Josie would do to embarrass her?

Josie tucked away her longings and refused to take offense. "I'd better go help clean up."

She started toward the gate.

"Is that all you had to say?" Margaretta asked. "You're lonely?"

"No, I'm fine, actually." Josie held her skirt with the hem above her shoes so she could walk through the grass quickly. "I've never been better."

Escaping, she calmed herself with a few deep breaths and a silent prayer for peace in her heart.

Darting through the long grasses, Anna scurried across her path with a wave and ran down the hill to join her friends. Anna must have mentioned inviting Josie along to her father, because Sam found Josie as soon as she returned. "You're welcome to come with us this afternoon."

"Thank you," she replied, prepared to decline the offer. But something made her turn and look at the woman still at the cemetery. An afternoon spent with the children would be an extraordinary distraction from her usual depressing routine. "The change of scenery will do me good. Where are you heading?"

"Henry asked me to visit the Dunlops. Seems the mister hasn't been to church for a while."

"That would be Ned. Eva and the children come pretty regularly."

The girls changed from their Sunday dresses while Josie went home and did the same. Sam simply removed his jacket, but wore his white shirt and tie. He settled a dun-colored hat on his head.

Josie hadn't been for a carriage ride in a long time. She sat on the front seat, with Anna between her and the preacher. Her straw hat shaded her eyes from the glare of the sun. Birds flew up from the brush. Deer mice and ground squirrels scampered across their path. Sam pointed out a pair of mule deer standing motionless on a ridge, as the land sloped downward and they approached a bridge.

For a moment, she had the illusion of what it might feel like to be part of a family, to have a kind and caring man as a husband. It was the kind of unrealistic daydream she tried not to entertain.

Anna grabbed her father's arm and spoke in a breathless panic, "Go back, Papa!"

Puzzled at the girl's sudden alarm, Josie shot her a glance.

"We've a lot more bridges to cross before we reach Colorado," Samuel replied. He set his mouth in a grim line.

"Please!" Anna begged and burst into tears. "Please go back! I want down now. Let me down!" She attempted to stand, but he restrained her with the back of his arm across her chest. She plopped back onto the seat, her distress real and her expression one of panic.

Confused, Josie looked from Anna to her father. He had his eyes on the road and the bridge ahead. "What's wrong, Anna?"

"Tell Papa to turn back! I don't want to go anymore." She burst into tears.

The sound of water running over stones reached Josie then, revealing the reason for Anna's distress. The water. Her mother had drowned crossing a river. The poor child was terrified.

"Come here," she said calmly, and wrapped her arm around Anna's quaking shoulders. "The bridge is perfectly safe. Half a dozen families crossed it on their way to church and home again just today."

Sobbing, Anna buried her face against Josie, and Josie held her as tightly as she could, covering her ears. A glance over her shoulder told her the other girls were white-lipped and distressed, as well, whether from the sound of the water or their sister's wailing, she couldn't be sure.

Anna's delicate body trembled, and her vulnerability sent empathy and concern spiraling straight to Josie's heart. Hot tears burned her eyes. "It's going to be all right now," she promised her. "We're almost there."

The carriage rattled the weathered boards as they crossed the river, and Anna trembled so violently, her teeth chattered. Josie cast a glance at Samuel. He was as tight-lipped as his daughters, though he wore determination like a shield.

Josie blinked away stinging tears. Anna's fear and the whole family's grief were so real to her at that moment that she felt their sorrow and anguish all the way to her bones.

The rattling stopped as they reached the ground on the other side. Josie loosened her tight hold and rubbed Anna's shoulder comfortingly. Eventually, the rushing sound of water faded into the distance and the only noise was the jingle of traces, the plodding of the horses and Anna's occasional sniff.

The child lowered her head to Josie's lap and lay with her eyes closed. Josie smoothed her hair away from her clammy face.

Josie wished she knew what to say to comfort this family. Finding no words, she silently prayed for the Lord to do it with His infinite love and mercy. The Harts deserved peace.

A few miles later, Josie broke the silence. "Oh, my goodness. I do believe those are real, live milk cows."

"Where?" Anna sat up and searched the landscape, spotting the brown and white cattle in a pasture. "I see 'em!"

The Dunlops' fields stretched on either side of the road, row after row of young corn and flourishing hay meadows. Chickens squawked and ran in a dozen directions when Sam pulled the carriage into the dooryard.

"Look at all them chickens," Anna cried, pointing.

"*Those* chickens," her father corrected.

He climbed down and assisted Anna, followed by her sisters, while on the other side, Josie used the step and hopped to the ground without help.

When he looked at her, Sam's expression conveyed his frustration and helplessness. She accepted his silent nod as approval for comforting his daughter. Josie gave him a hesitant smile.

Eva Dunlop came out of the small, square house, wiping her hands on her plain white apron.

"Mrs. Randolph, what a pleasure," she said with a warm smile. "Reverend Hart, I'm honored that you've called today. I can make fresh coffee."

"No call for that, ma'am. I was hoping to speak with your husband."

"He's in the barn."

Sam touched the brim of his hat with a courteous nod.

Elisabeth stepped up behind her father, but he stopped and turned to her. "Join the ladies this time."

She watched him walk away, her expression unreadable.

"Come on in," Eva said, gesturing to Josie and the girls. The Hart daughters followed the two women into the house.

The kitchen was tiny, with a well-worn table and four chairs. Rachel, who was about Elisabeth's age, turned from where she'd been kneading bread and studied the visitors. The girls stood waiting.

"Let's sit out of doors," Josie suggested. "It's too nice a day to waste inside, and you have a fine shade tree out there."

Sam introduced himself to Ned Dunlop. "I'm the interim preacher."

The man squinted through the rivulet of sweat that trickled into his eye as he leaned over a wagon wheel suspended on two sawhorses. "Preacher, huh?"

"Yes, sir."

Ned tugged a kerchief from the rear pocket of his denim pants and wiped sweat from his eyes. "You do anything besides preach?"

"Quite a lot of things actually. But the ministry is my calling and profession."

"Well, make yourself useful and sand that spoke there."

Sam rolled up his shirtsleeves. Picking up a spoke freshly crafted out of hard ash, he applied the sandpaper while Ned sawed another to the proper length. "Figured I'd replace all the old ones before they give out."

Once the spokes were all sanded, Sam helped him fit them into place around the hub.

Ned had propped the axle on a length of aged tree stump to hold up the wagon and remove the wheel. "That must've been quite a task alone. I'll help you get this back on."

"I keep that hunk of tree just for this," Ned told him. "Perfect height. Gotta grease the axle first." Had his tone made the task a challenge?

Sam spotted the pail of black grease with a foot-long paddle stuck in it. He stirred the muck to get a good amount and carried it to the axle.

Ned watched him smear it on the wood. Once Ned thought the job had been sufficiently accomplished, they set to working the wheel onto the axle and removing the stump at the same time.

Several grunts and a good deal of sweat later, they stood and wiped their faces on their sleeves.

Ned eyed Sam. "You been here over an hour, and you haven't said nigh a word about your Jesus."

Sam returned the look. "I showed you my Jesus."

"Y' think puttin' your back into my wagon will get me to church?"

Sam shrugged. "It's not my call to get you to church. I came to see what I could do for you."

Ned cast him a puzzled glance before turning toward the open doorway. "Gonna hitch up a team so I can take hay to the cows. This wagon's been out of commission for two days."

"It was a pleasure to meet you," Sam called after him.

Ned paused. "The missus will give you a cold drink before you head out." He met Sam's gaze briefly. "Appreciate the hand."

"Glad to be of help." Sam left the barn and approached the shade tree where the women sat on a blanket.

"There's a cake of lye soap and a pail of water on the porch, Reverend," Mrs. Dunlop called.

Josie looked up with surprise. A lock of Sam's dark hair had fallen over his brow, and he had grease streaked up both corded forearms. She suspected his damp white shirt would require special treatment at the laundry, but he looked more relaxed than she'd seen him since he'd arrived.

He washed, and Eva got him a jar of lemonade, which he drank thirstily before they said their goodbyes and headed out.

"How did your visit go?"

"Ned's a hardworking fellow. Didn't want to hinder his work, so I gave him a hand."

"Was he surprised?"

"Are you?"

His question caught her off guard. She didn't know why, but she had been surprised. "I guess I shouldn't have been."

His aware gaze edged to Anna seated between them. Josie suspected what he was thinking. Hoping to distract the child, she suggested, "Why don't we sing?"

Abigail joined her enthusiastically, and even Sam caught on and sang hymns in his deep baritone.

Not tricked, Anna watched the road with dread, seeing the bridge before she heard the water this time. Josie wrapped her arm around the child and tucked her tightly into her embrace, covering Anna's ears and continuing the song.

Anna cried and trembled, but she didn't beg her father to turn back. Perhaps she understood the bridge was the only way back to where they were staying. When the river was behind them, Josie loosened her hold and used her hem to wipe Anna's tears.

Sam's face had lost some of its healthy color, and Josie thought she noticed his hand tremble on the reins. Though he adjusted the brim of his hat and glanced across the waving prairie grass as though unaffected, she knew better.

Josie silently reminded the Lord about her prayers for the Hart family's comfort and strength and thanked Him for His love.

His daughter's distress ate a hole in his gut. Sam hated feeling helpless. It was because of him that his wife was gone and his children were miserable. Elisabeth's question haunted him every waking hour. Why hadn't God saved Carrie?

He'd prayed for their safety every morning and every night. He didn't believe God slept or turned a blind eye on His children. Sam should have been able to answer his daughter. He was a man of God.

But there was no good reason, no answer for why he'd left his wife lying in a barren patch of prairie he'd never see again. Her burial place had blended into the countryside as though she'd never existed. Carrie was lost to him forever.

He felt sick at the fact that she wasn't buried near her parents, or even in a decent place, with shade trees and a marker; but then he forced himself to remember she had gone on to be with Jesus and was walking on streets of gold right at that moment.

His lofty plans mocked him. Life had to go on without her. Now that his children were motherless and he was a widower, he second-guessed his choices. If he hadn't wanted to come west…

Anna's sobs took him back to the hoarse convulsive sounds she'd made the day they'd stood over Carrie's grave. Her wet braids had thumped against her back with each burst of tears. Elisabeth had trembled so violently, her teeth had chattered. Abigail had grasped Anna and held her tightly, even though shock was plain on her red-blotched face.

Only the previous night, he and Carrie had sat beside the fire and talked about their new home. That morning had been like every other on the trail—no sense of impending disaster, no forewarning of the tragedy that was about to devastate their family.

Regret and misery had squeezed Sam's chest until he didn't know how his heart could still beat.

Why didn't God save her? Elisabeth's heartbroken question had sliced through Sam's cocoon of shock.

And now Anna's ragged breaths reminded him of all the suffering and loss he was helpless to change.

"Would you girls like to come to my house in the morning?" Josie asked. "I'll be preparing for the ladies to come quilting on Tuesday. I would enjoy your company and your help."

Her lighthearted question brought Sam out of his reverie and into the present. For a brief moment he almost resented that it was her sitting on the other side of Anna on the wagon seat and not his wife, but he corrected himself. Josie was exactly what all of them needed right now.

"I want to come!" Anna responded immediately.

"What do you need help doing?" Abigail asked.

"A little sweeping and dusting," Josie answered, and then grinned. "Oh, and I almost forgot. There are cookies and teacakes to make."

Abigail squealed. "Yes! I love to bake!"

Sam met Josie's gaze and read the pleasure in those amber depths. She truly enjoyed his daughters. The knowledge eased the ache in his chest. *Thank You, Lord.*

Josie glanced back at Elisabeth, but Sam's oldest daughter said nothing.

"What about you, Elisabeth?" he asked.

"I have reading to do."

Josie looked away, but not before Sam detected hurt. Elisabeth needed more time. And he had to believe that time would be a healer for all of them.

Chapter Seven

On Monday morning, Abigail and Anna left Elisabeth studying and walked to Josie's.

"We'll write these recipes in your journal," Josie told Abigail as they measured butter and cut it into sugar to make dough for wafer cookies. "Then you can make them yourselves when you get to Colorado."

Abigail paused with her hand on the wooden spoon. Josie glanced over to catch a flicker of pain crossing her expression.

She lifted Abigail's chin on floury fingers and looked into her eyes. "Your life is going to be different than planned, isn't it?"

The girl nodded.

Josie released her chin, but Abigail continued to look at her, as though waiting for help or encouragement. Though she felt inadequate, Josie was compelled to offer what she could.

"Sometimes it feels like we can't get through things. Like it's too hard to go on. But we keep going because people depend on us. And we grow stronger than we ever thought we could be."

Abigail nodded. "Papa says the joy of the Lord is our strength."

"Your papa's a wise man. And he loves you very much."

Anna hopped down from where she'd been stirring eggs at the table and stood beside her sister. Her wide hazel eyes were filled with concern. "I don't think there's enough joy to make me not scared of the river."

Josie didn't know what to say that would help a nine-year-old conquer a fear like that. She and her sisters had been swept away by a swift current, and that had been terrifying. And the river had taken her mother's life. "What does your papa say about that?"

"He doesn't say anything about it. I think he's kinda scared, too."

Josie doubted he was as afraid of water as he was of how he was going to raise three daughters without a mother. "When I don't have an answer," Josie told her, "and I don't know what to do, I ask God to show me the way."

"And does He?"

"He promised never to leave us or forsake us," she replied. "And He said we could always trust Him. So I do." Josie placed her cutting board on the table and instructed Anna to sprinkle flour on it. "Now we work the dough until it's smooth, and then let it stand."

"Elisabeth is missing all the good times," Abigail said softly.

It was obvious that Elisabeth resented Josie and every attempt she made to befriend the girls. Josie was only happy to help make their lives more pleasant. They'd been through so much and had lived in trying conditions along the trail. They'd be back at it soon enough, and she only hoped to ease their burdens during the time they were here.

"Can we be here when your friends come to-morrow?" Anna asked.

"It's not polite to invite your own self," Abigail scolded.

"I was going to invite you," Josie said kindly. "I just didn't know if you'd want to spend the morning with a bunch of chatty ladies, while they sew and drink tea."

"Oh, I do!" Anna assured her.

Josie looked at Abigail, who nodded with a hopeful smile.

"Of course you're welcome. We'll ask Elisabeth to join us, too. The ladies will enjoy your company. Have any of you ever quilted?"

They shook their heads.

"But we liked tea parties in Philadelphia," Abigail assured her.

"Well, I'll make some practice squares for you,

and you can watch how it's done and try your hand with the needle and thread."

"And eat cookies!" Anna said emphatically.

They turned their attention to their task.

That evening at supper, the two younger girls chattered about their day and anticipated the following morning's event.

With assistance, Reverend Martin had made it to the dining room to sit at the table with them.

"Elisabeth, I'd like it very much if you joined us in the morning," Josie told her.

Elisabeth glanced at Samuel. "What will you be doing in the morning, Father?"

"I'm counseling the young couple I'll be marrying next weekend. You go and enjoy yourself with the ladies and your sisters."

"Thank you, Mrs. Randolph. I accept your invitation." Her tone didn't reflect much joy.

Samuel smiled at her approvingly.

Elisabeth's desire to please her father was evident in all she said and did. Josie recognized her need for approval, and she appreciated Sam's attention to his daughters.

There was a rap at the back door. Josie dabbed her lips with her napkin and went to answer it.

"Brought a load of wood," James told her. He stood holding am armful of neatly chopped limbs.

She stepped back. "We're just eating supper. Will you join us?"

"Yes'm." He arranged the pieces of wood so they fit in the bin beside the stove, then hung his cap on a hook.

She handed him a stack of dessert plates and picked up the pie. "James," she said once they'd reached the other room. "These are the Harts. This is our friend, James Lester," she told them. "He's my checker chum, aren't you, James?"

The fourteen-year-old glanced at the sisters. Without a reply, he ducked his head and took a seat on the chair that Josie scooted closer for him.

She dished slices of dried apple pie onto the plates and Elisabeth stood to pass one to each person.

James thanked her without meeting her eyes.

Anna, never at a loss for words or questions, spoke up. "Do you live close? Do you go to school here? Are there lots of girls in your class? Is your teacher nice?"

"Me and my ma live on top o' the barbershop," he answered.

"I never heard of anyone living on top of a barbershop," Anna said. "Is it a long way up?"

"Anna, let James eat his pie," Samuel said, with an apologetic glance at the boy.

"Why don't you stay this evening?" Josie suggested. She looked at the sisters. "We never learned if any of you are checker players."

"Father and I used to play in the evening when we lived in Philadelphia," Elisabeth answered.

"We'll take turns, then," Josie said.

"I wanna learn!" Anna piped up.

"I have a board and disks at my house in a closet," Josie told her.

Josie and her chattering little friend took a walk in the cool of the early evening, pausing to wave to Alice Iverson, who sat on her front porch with her children. Josie felt a sense of purpose this evening. The melancholy feeling she normally experienced when she saw Alice and her youngsters remained blissfully at bay.

When they returned, Reverend Martin gave Josie a tender smile, reminding her he was still waiting for her reply.

"Can I bring you anything?" she asked.

"Not until my coffee later," he answered. "I'll be glad when I'm able to do something for you, for a change. You deserve the return of kindness."

Uncharacteristic warmth climbed her cheeks, the thought that she was blushing embarrassing her all the more. But no one seemed to notice, and she showed Anna how to set up the pieces on the checkerboard.

Josie and James played at a small table, while Elisabeth and her father shared a game on the ottoman. Anna bobbed back and forth between both games, asking questions.

"She'll catch on quickly once she plays," Josie predicted.

Elisabeth captured Sam's last king, and they waited while Josie and James finished their game.

Josie moved down to oppose Anna, and Elisabeth seated herself at the table with James.

Abigail sat beside her father on the sofa, and he wrapped an arm around her. Josie caught herself watching them, instead of making suggestions for Anna's moves. Abigail looked at him with such adoration, and he absently rubbed the back of her hand. Josie thought of all the evenings she'd sat alone, waiting for her father to return, only to have him breeze past on his way to the next place.

She shook off her discontentment. Her father had been an important man who helped a lot of people acquire justice. He'd loved her and provided for her, leaving her well off after his death. She had much to be grateful for.

Reverend Martin had to remind her when it was her turn to move.

The evening wore on and Anna got tired, yawning behind her hand. Samuel took her up to bed, allowing the other two girls another game if they wanted one. James and Elisabeth played again, while Reverend Martin took on Abigail by sliding the ottoman close to the chair where he sat. Josie watched contentedly. She couldn't remember a time when her days had been so full and she'd felt such accomplishment at the end of the evening.

Samuel returned, taking a seat. His interested gaze rested on Elisabeth and James. Earlier, they'd behaved awkwardly with each other, avoiding eye contact and speaking rarely. Now Elisabeth's shy smiles and the nervous bouncing of James's knee under the table hinted of age-old boy-meets-girl chemistry.

They seemed so young to Josie, and they were. She barely remembered being Elisabeth's age.

Much later, after James had gone home and the girls had scampered up to bed, Sam assured her he would see to the reverend's needs. The two men planned to talk a while longer.

"Good evening, then." Josie checked the stove before heading home.

A movement on the other side of the street surprised her, and a slender figure stepped out of the shadows into the moonlight. "Hello, Mrs. Randolph."

"James! What are you doing out so late?"

"My mother isn't off work yet, so I was walkin' until it's time to get her. I like to walk her home."

"That's nice of you. I'm sure she appreciates it, but maybe you should stay a little closer to the café."

"It's all right. I can walk you home if you want."

"Okay."

"Elisabeth is smart. She beat me at checkers twice."

"You didn't let her win?"

"Maybe once."

Josie laughed. They paused in front of her house. "Why don't you come for supper tomorrow evening?"

"Thanks, Mrs. Randolph!" James grinned and spun to leave.

Smiling, she climbed the stairs to her home.

Josie couldn't have put her feelings into words the following morning as she and Abigail draped her dining room table with a heavy lace cloth. With her tongue poking out of the corner of her mouth in concentration, Anna carried trays of cookies and tea cakes into the room.

As Josie took the last one from her, Elisabeth joined them. "I've arranged the chairs in a big circle, as you asked."

Josie loved having the girls in her home, enjoyed hearing their chatter. Planning this day and carrying it out was an experience like none she had known. Their mother must have felt so blessed and been so proud. What did it feel like to have brought fresh new lives into the world? To nurture and love them and watch them grow into sweet children and pretty young ladies?

She'd never wanted anything more than to know how that felt. But her dreams of family and children had slowly and painfully faded—dying altogether with Bram.

She shook off her gloomy thoughts, opting to make the most of every minute with the girls. "I've never been prepared this early."

The sisters had dressed in their Sunday frocks, Elisabeth's a bright blue that brought out the vivid color of her eyes, Abigail's a deep violet that set off her shining, pale hair and Anna's a lemony yellow that made her hazel eyes appear darker.

"These were our last new dresses," Abigail said, glancing at Elisabeth's hem, which was already a trifle short.

"I might be able to let that down for you," Josie told the eldest sister.

"Most likely, Father will take us to the seamstress when we reach Colorado," Elisabeth answered.

"Papa said we'd be making the best of our clothing," Abigail reminded her. "You should let Josie take down the hem."

"I could do it myself."

"I think you can," Josie agreed. "I could show you how to hem it evenly, if you like." She understood that Elisabeth had taken over the mothering position for her sisters. Apparently, their fondness for Josie— and Josie's help—threatened her in some way. Her prickliness over Josie's involvement stemmed from losing her mother.

Josie didn't want to be pushy, so she let the subject drop.

Always curious, Anna asked, "How did your dad—I mean—um—how did your Mr. Randolph die?"

"My *husband*," Josie supplied, "ran the newspaper office. He set all those tiny letters that make up the print into trays." She arranged her silver forks in a shiny, cascading row as she spoke. "He started having bad headaches, so painful that he often came home and went to bed. Light hurt his eyes, so I had to make the room dark with heavy draperies." Those had been difficult times, and the memories weren't pleasant. "After a few months, he lost his vision—"

"Did you help him find it?" Anna asked.

"That means he couldn't see," Abigail told her.

"That's right." Josie nodded. "It wasn't long until he died. The doctor believed he had a growth in his head. I'm afraid we'll never know for sure."

"Who puts the tiny letters into the trays now?" Anna asked.

"Well, I inherited the newspaper," Josie told her. "But I have no idea how to run it, nor do I want to learn, so I took a partner. A man by the name of Carlisle bought half. I don't know if he does the typesetting himself, or if he hired a helper."

"I'm sad for you," Anna told her with sympathy in her expression.

"Don't be sad for me," Josie answered. "I have lots of friends, and I stay very busy."

"I think you should get a new dad," Anna stated.

"Husband," Elisabeth corrected.

"I might just do that one of these days," Josie said with a smile. The bell on the door grated, effectively ending their conversation. "Here we go!"

Grace and Becka Hulbert were the first to arrive, followed by several others. The quilting ladies were pleased to have the Hart girls join them. Grace asked the sisters numerous questions about themselves and their father. Josie had already experienced the woman's interest in the newly widowed preacher as a prospect for her daughter, and the other ladies picked up on it right away.

"Grace, let the children work on their practice squares," Mrs. Wilbur admonished her in a deliberately good-natured tone, and then launched into a commentary on the marigolds she'd planted around the edge of her tomato garden. "They're going to keep the rabbits away."

Nettie laughed. "You're going to need more than marigolds, Pauline."

Josie helped the girls with their squares, showing them the embroidery stitches. As with everything, Elisabeth displayed skill and precision with hers. Abigail chose variegating colors and Anna liked red. Even the leaves on her rose were red. Elisabeth pointed out that they should have been green, but Josie and Abigail assured Anna that any color she liked was beautiful and just right for her square.

"Maybe we can make a quilt for Papa's bed," Abigail suggested.

All three girls fell silent.

Josie glanced from one to the other. None of them met her gaze. "Is something wrong?"

Elisabeth shook her head. Anna got tears in her eyes.

"What is it?" Josie asked, kneeling in front of the youngest child and placing her hand over Anna's.

"Our mama was wrapped up in the wedding

quilt when we—when she—when we left her behind," Anna said.

Behind Josie, the ladies became uncomfortably silent.

Chapter Eight

By the looks on the ladies' faces, Josie was certain their hearts went out to these girls just as hers did.

Seeing the children's pain, Josie wanted to cry, too. But she squeezed Anna's hand. She knew the grief of losing a mother.

The ladies murmured, more than one sniffed, and their quilting resumed. Josie assured the girls that they could work on quilt squares as often as they liked, and she would even help them if they wanted to take on the project of making a quilt for their father.

Together they served refreshments, and after the ladies went home, the sisters helped Josie clean up. These girls needed a woman in their lives. She prayed that once they reached their destination and settled into their new church, that time would heal the wounds and they would welcome a new wife for their father. Of course, it wouldn't be the same as having their own mother, but any woman would be blessed to marry into their family.

At the thought of Samuel caring enough for a woman to marry again—and the idea of the girls lending their affections to that wife—Josie's heart skipped an erratic beat. She had become involved. She cared about them. Her life was going to be unbearably quiet and empty when they left.

Josie's chest ached at the prospect, so she cast her thoughts aside, to be concerned with only today. They'd come into her lives for a season, and she was determined to enjoy it.

At supper that evening, Sam appreciated the animation with which Anna and Abigail spoke about their afternoon. Even Elisabeth smiled once or twice, adding a remark to the conversation. Their talk of embroidering and eating ginger cookies held more normalcy than anything had in the past months.

He had Josie to thank for that.

The girls didn't have to be reminded to help clear the table. Reverend Martin talked about a tornado that had passed through a few years previous, and Sam listened with interest.

After finishing his coffee, he picked up his cup and the reverend's to carry them into the kitchen.

Josie was speaking softly, and he heard his wife mentioned, so he paused just outside the doorway and peered in.

All three girls and Josie were seated at one end of the kitchen table, as though Josie had gathered them there.

Josie held Anna's hand and looked directly into her eyes. "It's a good thing to remember your mama," she told her, and then included the other two with her warm gaze. "We keep people alive in our hearts by remembering the good times and the love we shared when we were together."

A shard of pain pierced Sam's heart, quickly followed by a flash of anger. Who was this woman to address such a difficult subject? His children didn't need their wounds reopened.

"I missed my mother terribly for a long time. But now when I think of her, I think of all the ways she made me laugh. I remember our evenings together by the fire."

Sam strained to see his daughter's expressions. Anna's face had lit up and she listened intently.

"What's the best time you can remember having with your mother?" Josie turned her gaze. "Abigail?"

Unbelievably, Abigail's eyes brightened. "We went to the theater and watched a ballet before Christmas."

Sam's surprise was so great he had to focus on not dropping the cups he held.

"On the way home," Abigail continued, "we stopped for hot chocolate. It was snowing, and Mama was so pretty in her black wool coat and fur muff."

Similar images sabotaged Sam's mind. Carrie had been so young and lovely.

"That's a wonderful memory." He tore his attention back to the scene before him. Josie turned to Elisabeth, and Sam's heart nearly exploded. "What about you, sweetie? Do you recall a good time with your mother?"

Sam didn't believe his oldest daughter would answer, but she studied her sisters' faces and replied, "Sitting in church every Sunday morning. Mother was so proud of Father."

Sam could hardly breathe.

"She watched him with a special look on her face," Elisabeth added. "And she was the prettiest lady there."

Abigail and Anna nodded.

Those were the times and the days he'd robbed them of. Those were the things they'd never get back.

"That's awfully nice, Elisabeth." Josie turned to Anna. "What about you?"

Sam's heart melted as he waited for his youngest child to share something about her mother.

"Mama used to give me a baff and wash my hair, and then we'd sit by the stove and she'd brush it dry. She told me about when she was a little girl and Grandmama dried her hair by the fire." Anna paused for a thoughtful moment. "Elisabeth helps me wash my hair now."

"Elisabeth's a good sister." Josie smiled and

released Anna's hands. "Thank you for sharing your good memories."

They were silent a moment, but then Abigail said, "Talking about her made me sad, but it was a different kind of sad. I miss her, but if I remember the good times it's not so hard."

"It's good to talk about her," Josie assured them. "It's good to think of her and remember how much she loved you. You are blessed to share those memories with each other. You'll always have them in common."

The girls glanced at one another with hesitant smiles.

"I'm gonna draw a picture of Mama," Anna announced.

Josie stood. "Why don't you all run along now and enjoy your evening reading…or drawing. I'll finish up here."

Advising them to think of pleasant times should have come from him, but how could he lead anyone somewhere he'd never gone? Realizing he would be discovered eavesdropping if he didn't move, Sam collected himself and stepped into the kitchen.

Anna spotted him and ran over to hug him around the waist. "I'm gonna draw a picture of Mama."

Josie hurried toward him and took the cups, so his hands were free.

"I'll be up in a little while, and we'll read together."

With a clamber of shoes and a whirl of skirts, they

were gone, leaving him to face the woman he'd had unkind thoughts about only moments ago. Guilt engulfed him at his quick leap to anger when he'd heard her mention his wife. *Forgive me, Lord.*

Her intentions were pure and kind. His daughters had opened up to her with stories of their mother in a surprisingly forthcoming manner. What did he know about little girls? What did he know about losing a mother? Josie Randolph apparently knew about both and cared enough to counsel them. He studied her as she checked the steaming teakettle. He'd noticed that she was a lovely woman, of course, but he hadn't looked at her as anything other than Henry's helper.

He appreciated that she'd been a blessing to his distraught family, but he took a moment now to appreciate her dark, shiny hair and the curve of her ivory cheek. She'd lost someone just as he had, and for the first time he wondered about her grief and loneliness.

He reached for a stack of dishes. "Let me help."

"I can do this." She waved her free hand. "You go read with the girls."

"Actually, I wanted a moment alone with you."

"Oh?" The squeaky syllable showed her surprise. As did the way she quickly and efficiently shaved soap into the enamel dishpan. "What can I do for you, Reverend?"

How like her to ask. He shook his head. "You've done so much already. I want you to know I recognize your care and concern. I appreciate everything. More than you can know."

Obviously uncomfortable with his praise, she lowered her lashes and absently skimmed the edge of the table with her index finger. "They're lovely young ladies. So different from one another."

She raised her caramel-brown gaze to his. Surely the affection he thought he felt for her at that moment was only appreciation. He didn't have it in him to feel more. He didn't want to feel more.

He had so much turmoil on his heart that he couldn't sort through it to find adequate words. Perhaps there simply weren't any. "Their mother doted on them. Took care of everything."

She picked up a towel. "The loss must be difficult for all of you."

"I guess," he said, pausing to study her, "that you know about loss yourself. You lost your husband."

She nodded and answered simply, "Yes."

"How did you do it?" he asked. "Go on with your life after that? How did you bear the days and nights without him?"

A flicker of pain creased her brow.

"I'm sorry. That was too forward of me."

"No, it wasn't, Sam. It's an honest concern. I just don't know if I have a helpful answer. I didn't do anything particularly brave or wise. I just got up and made every day count somehow. I didn't want to lose myself." Her rich caramel-colored eyes beseeched him to understand.

And he did—because he had lost something of himself.

Overwhelmed with confusion, he nodded. He wanted so much for them. He'd had a vision for his family that had never taken this daunting possibility into consideration. He felt sorely inadequate for the task laid out before him. "I understand," he said softly.

"You're fortunate to have your children," she told him. "To still have a family."

"I am blessed," he replied.

"And you recognize your blessing. With all you have to do, you make time for your daughters," she said almost reverently. "They know you love them and they can tell that they're important to you. You make them feel safe."

Sam stared blindly at the dishes on the table for a moment. How could she think that? Anna's terror nearly tore his heart out. Abigail's nightmares were most likely the same horrifying images he dreamed. And Elisabeth didn't even seem like herself anymore. He shook his head.

Josie had the feeling she'd said too much. Using the towel to protect her hands, she poured hot water from the teakettle and set it back on the stove. After adding cooler water, she lowered a stack of plates into the suds. There were things she'd observed that she wasn't comfortable mentioning. Abigail's beseeching looks when Elisabeth accompanied her father, for one. But Josie wasn't a part of their family, and she had no business meddling.

Samuel's presence had become disconcerting. More often than not when he was near, she found herself thinking about the wave in his near-black hair or the clean, solid line of his jaw. He was a tall, broad-shouldered man, but he moved with a fluid agility and masculine grace she couldn't help but appreciate. She reminded herself that he was a widower, a father and a preacher. Besides those facts, she was considering marrying Reverend Martin.

"I just meant to say thank you," he said, finally looking up.

"I'm just making every day count," she replied.

"Don't minimize your importance or my gratitude."

"All right. You're welcome."

One corner of his mouth turned up and the atmosphere between them changed. She would probably float if he turned on a full-fledged smile. She was unaccustomed to the buoyant sensation—but she liked it.

With that, he turned and left the room. Josie let her hands fall still in the dishwater as she pictured him going upstairs, Abigail sitting close to him, and Anna squirming onto his lap. The empty feeling that image created forced her to turn her thoughts in a new direction.

She was supposed to be giving thought to Reverend Mar—*Henry's* proposal. Why was it she had to work to focus on the issue, to even consider the possibility? Henry was a kind man who served the Lord with all his heart. He would make a good companion, and she needed companionship.

Give me wisdom, Lord. "I want to make the right choice," she prayed softly. "I don't want to be alone, but I want to fulfill Your purpose for my life, so please show me what You would have me do."

Josie finished the dishes. Her talk with the girls had brought back memories of her childhood and the time she'd spent with her mother. Her mother must have missed her husband. Josie realized that she had probably been a comfort to her mother during those long days and nights while her father traveled. At least, she hoped so. A child would have been a blessing to *her,* had she been able to have one.

Somehow, her thoughts had come full circle. Josie wiped the last plate and turned down the wall lamps. She found Henry in his study with his Bible open on his lap. He sat with his chin resting on his knuckles, his elbow on the arm on the chair. His smile greeted her.

She stood for a moment, clasping her hands in front of her. She should have something more to say to him. She felt bad for not having a ready answer. The prospect of becoming his wife had changed the once-easy rapport they'd shared.

"Is everything all right?" he asked.

She nodded. "Fine. I'm tired. I'll see you in the morning."

She shouldn't have been relieved to go home. Normally, she stayed until it grew late. Closing the door behind her, she strolled out onto the brick walkway and turned to look up at the light in the bedroom window. A few words of the hymn she so often thought of came to her lips.

"Be still, my soul: thy God doth undertake
to guide the future as He has the past.
Thy hope, thy confidence let nothing shake;
and now mysterious shall be bright at last."

God was in control of her future, and in that she could place her trust and confidence. She prayed to be sensitive to His leading and to hear clearly when He guided her decision.

"I'm listening, Lord. I'm listening."

In a clear voice, Elisabeth read a particularly exciting chapter of *Alice's Adventures in Wonderland*. Carrie had purchased the novel the year it was published, and they'd read it through a half dozen times since. This was only Anna's second time to hear the story.

Elisabeth sat on the end of the bed, her slender bare feet dangling above the wood floor, her long, thick hair cascading over her shoulders.

Sam sat in a comfortable chair only a few feet away, with Abigail at his feet and Anna perched on his lap. His concentration wavered as the image of the three of them gathered at the kitchen table sharing memories of their mother sharpened his already overworked conscience.

The overwhelming need to fix what he'd done to

them never went away. He had their futures to think of, a life to build for them, and now a secondary plan had to come from scratch.

He held so much self-recrimination and doubt inside that he didn't have the ability to draw his children out the way Josie had tonight. He should have been the one helping them remember their mother. He should have been the one assuring his girls that their grief was a normal thing. But he hadn't been. Instead, he continued to let them down.

Hearing their conversation, seeing their faces and Josie's genuine concern had been hard to accept at first. But now, after he'd had time to absorb it, he saw that she could do for them what he couldn't.

They needed someone to guide them, someone to nurture and care for them. Only a woman understood feminine mysteries and only a woman could fill that place in their lives.

Maybe in the back of his mind, he'd imagined that once they were settled in Colorado and had a home, he might find them a mother. But he hadn't truly allowed a complete thought to form, because that would have been disloyal to Carrie.

His daughters needed a woman to teach them things like embroidery and cooking. A woman could help them develop into proper young women.

His mind raced. At first his thoughts were so shocking, he didn't want to entertain them, but once he gave himself over to the possibility, the idea seemed perfect.

He needed a helpmate. His children needed a mother. Josie was levelheaded and lovely, the picture of an ideal woman. She was a pleasant companion and a strong woman of God. Granted, he hadn't known her long, but he'd never heard a cross word from her, and had seen only her kindness and generosity.

Josie was a widow. She had no children of her own. She was everything the girls needed, and she already cared about them.

She was the perfect answer.

Chapter Nine

He had the answer.

Sam couldn't change the past, nor could he replace Carrie, but he could fix things by securing this perfect woman to take care of his children.

A weight in his chest gave him pause. What would Carrie think? Would she approve?

Sam had asked God to help him through this time. He prayed continually for direction and wisdom and strength. At that moment, he understood that Josie was the answer to his prayers. Carrie would approve.

Anna yawned as Elisabeth ended the chapter.

He kissed the top of Anna's head. "Get yourselves into bed now."

Elisabeth made herself comfortable on the narrow cot, and the other two snuggled into the bigger bed. Sam kissed each of them. "I love you," he said with emotion making his words thick in his throat.

"I love you," they echoed.

His feet barely touched the stairs. Henry had already taken himself off to bed, so Sam checked the fireplace and stove and let himself out of doors.

Anna had shown him which street Josie lived on, and he hurried, seeking the house she'd described. In the dark, he wasn't sure if he'd be able to find it. This probably hadn't been a good idea, but he'd been eager to set things in motion. He reached the end of the block and started back toward the parsonage.

"Good evening, Reverend," a male voice called out.

Sam stopped before a two-story home with a wide porch.

A form separated from the shadows.

He recognized Reggie Iverson and stretched out a hand in greeting. "The missus and I are real pleased that you're here. It's good to have church again."

"I'm enjoying the people of Durham," Sam told him honestly. "And there are a lot of excellent cooks among the wives."

They chatted a few minutes longer. Sam had pretty much given up on finding Josie's house that night.

"Josie lets us pick apples from her backyard." Reggie turned aside and gestured. "Alice makes apple dumplings that melt in your mouth. If you're here for the season, she'll cook some up for you."

Sam's attention had once again been captured. "Mrs. Randolph has apple trees?"

"A whole row of fine ones," Reggie replied. "Lives right there, she does. Shame Bram died so young and left her on her own. He must be gone… oh, three or four years now. Ran the newspaper, her husband did."

"I'll look forward to those dumplings."

The man turned and walked toward his house and let himself inside. Sam observed as the door blocked out the light, then he studied Josie's house in the dark.

A solitary light shone from an upstairs window.

He loped across the lawn without bothering to take the walkway and leaped the stairs three at a time to reach her door. He groped and found a metal knob to twist, hoping the grating noise didn't alert the neighbors.

Sam ran his palms along his thighs and waited.

Finally, the door opened. A light behind Josie outlined her loose hair and her slender form in a wrapper. "Reverend Hart?" Quickly, she stepped out onto the porch. "What's wrong? Is it Henry?"

"No, no. Henry's fine." Anticipating her next question, he added, "The girls are fine. I—need to speak with you."

Her pause was barely discernible. "All right." She glanced at the doorway. "Do you want to come in?"

"We can talk out here."

She pulled the door closed and stood in front of him.

Sam glanced around and spotted wicker chairs at the other end of the porch. "Let's sit."

She padded in front of him and took a seat. Sam lowered himself to the chair opposite.

Here, the moonlight was bright enough to see her smooth features and the sheen of her dark hair. She waited expectantly. It was highly unusual for him to call at this hour of the evening—or to call at all. "Did I get you out of bed?"

"No. I've been sewing upstairs and had just changed my clothes."

A silent moment passed. Beyond the Iversons' hedge, a cat yowled. She must be wondering what in creation brought him here, and already he wasn't doing a very good job of this.

"Please don't think me presumptuous," he began. "Is there anything…any*one* tethering you to this place? To Nebraska?"

She changed her position on the chair. "Durham has always been my home. But I don't have any family, if that's what you mean. Except, of course, my husband's mother." She glanced aside. "I have this house."

"Would you ever consider leaving?"

She shrugged. "I don't know. I've never thought about it. There's never been any reason."

"What about starting over? Would that be a good reason?"

Josie studied what she could see of Samuel Hart's face in the shadows of the porch. His questions were puzzling, though she was trying to make sense of them and follow his train of thought. Starting over where? "I-I'm not sure."

"Josie, I'm thinking that you and I could make a new start together."

He had her interest now!

"I want to do the very best I can for my family. I want to make up to them for what I've put them through. You're so good with my daughters."

A new start somewhere else? Her mind shot back to those words. "What are you saying?"

"I would be honored if you would marry me and come to Colorado with us," he said.

The night sounds faded into the silent cocoon of her whirling mind, and his words took over her thinking. Astonishment stole her breath. Marry him? He'd asked her to marry him?

He was handsome and smart. She'd witnessed his tenderness toward his children, listened to his strong words of love as he preached straight from the Word of God. This imposing and fascinating man sitting on her porch had proposed to her!

Her heart raced against her ribs.

Josie pressed her hand to her chest and let her thoughts settle. *I would be honored if you would marry me and come to Colorado with us.*

She thought of her earlier prayer for wisdom in making choices. God knew she didn't want to be alone, but she'd hesitated over Henry's proposal. Perhaps this was why she'd been unable to make that commitment.

The irony struck her, and she couldn't hold back a chuckle. "Oh, Lord, You do work in mysterious ways."

"What are you thinking?" Sam asked.

She was thinking that she'd been unable to give Reverend Martin an answer because God had something else planned. He was offering her more than a companion.

Sam had suggested a new beginning together. And God was providing the family she'd so desperately yearned for. Emotion welled within her and hot tears flooded her eyes. "I'm thinking I would love to marry you and move to Colorado to start over."

Sam released a pent-up breath and leaned out of his chair to engulf her in a hearty hug.

Startled, Josie returned the embrace, enjoying the warmth, breathing in his scent, a combination of clean clothing and bay rum. God had deemed to give her an affectionate husband after all. And children, as well! Her heart brimmed to overflowing. God's mercy and kindness knew no bounds.

Sam released her to stand and take a step back as though realizing the impropriety of hugging her on her porch.

He reached for her hand, and she took his.

"Father," he said, his voice low and reverent. "Thank You for Your grace and mercy. Thank You for setting my feet on the path of righteousness and pointing me in the direction You'd have me take. I've made mistakes in the past, but I only want to hear Your voice. I know if I trust in You, You will bless this family we are creating to serve You."

His earnestly spoken words touched Josie so

deeply she could scarcely breathe. She appreciated the way he spoke to God, as though he was having a conversation, and that thanking God had been the first thing on his mind.

"Help me be the man You want me to be, and give Josie all the strength and love she's going to need for the weeks and months ahead. I ask in Jesus' name. Amen."

"Amen," Josie said around the emotion thickening her voice. *Thank You for this man,* she wanted to add, but her voice wouldn't work.

He backed to the stairs. "You'll have things to take care of to get ready. I'll help you in any way I can."

"I-I'll have to sell my house." And her share of the newspaper. And tell Henry her decision. And Margaretta. She pressed both palms to her hot cheeks. "Oh, my."

"Is selling your house a problem?"

She got up and followed him to the stairs. "Not at all. I'm just feeling a bit overwhelmed."

"We'll have a ceremony before we leave for Colorado," he continued.

She nodded. She would have to decide what to do with all of her belongings. "I need time to tell a few people."

"Of course. We'll wait long enough for that, and then we'll tell the girls together. This is a good plan," he said.

Josie didn't think "good" was descriptive enough for the new surge of hope that swelled in her heart.

"It's a lot to think about right now, but with God's blessing, what more could we ask?"

Sam glanced aside and then at her. He descended a couple of steps. "I'd—ah—I'd better go. Good night." He turned and jogged down the rest of the stairs.

She strained to watch him until his tall form blended with the night and he was gone. Wrapping her arms around herself, she returned to sink onto the chair in a state of awe.

She was going to be Samuel Hart's wife!

Her head filled with images of the new life they would build, of the beautiful mountain country she'd never dreamed to see. She would prepare their home and fill it with loving touches. She would be a loving and devoted wife, and she wouldn't expect too much from her husband. He was a busy man who put God first and had his ministry and his daughters to concern himself with.

Josie imagined helping Abigail and Anna with their homework and their hair. She could buy patterns and make them new dresses. Elisabeth would warm to her. Josie would never replace their mother, of course, but she could fill a place of need and become an important thread in their lives.

She would be part of the Hart family. Josie Hart. When they arrived in Colorado, she would be at Sam's side as they met the new congregation.

She barely slept that night, exhilarating thoughts of her new life swirling through her mind, and eventually in her dreams.

* * *

The next morning reality barely dimmed her fantasies. She hummed as she prepared breakfast. The girls looked prettier than ever, and when Sam entered the kitchen in his black trousers and white shirt, the sight took her breath away and joy rose in her heart. She gave him a secret smile and turned away before one of his daughters noticed.

"Good morning," he said from behind her. "Did you sleep well?"

She'd barely slept a wink. "Yes, thanks. And you?"

"I slept better than I have since we arrived here."

She turned back with a plate of fried potatoes. "Have you checked on Reverend Martin?"

"He shaved and dressed himself."

"He's getting stronger every day. I think your family has been good for him. And you've taken away the burden he felt about letting down his flock."

The man they'd been discussing appeared in the doorway. "What's that I smell? Is it bacon?"

"And corn-bread muffins," Josie replied.

"What's the special occasion?" Henry asked, stiffly seating himself at the head of the table.

Josie quickly turned back to the stove. The thought of disappointing him stabbed her with dismay. The last thing she wanted was to let him down or—even worse—hurt him.

"Where are you going today?" Elisabeth asked her father.

"I have a telegram to send, and I need to make a visit to the bank and the farrier. Then I'll be studying in the church."

"May I go on your errands with you?" his oldest daughter asked.

"Why don't all of you come with me for the morning? We'll leave Mrs. Randolph to her tasks, and Reverend Martin can listen to the silence."

Henry laughed. "I have plenty of quiet time. Don't worry about me."

Everyone was in a good mood while they ate. Josie declined help for the dishes, and Sam and his daughters left.

Sometime later, Josie took another cup of coffee to the reverend's study, but he wasn't there. Surprised, she walked through the house. Glancing out the front window, she spotted him on the porch.

He thanked her for the coffee and took a sip. "For a while there, I wasn't sure I'd be seeing the sun again."

She perched on the porch rail, facing him. A falling sensation in her stomach betrayed her nervousness, but she couldn't hesitate.

He set down his cup.

"Henry," she began, still uncomfortable with his given name. "I've made a decision."

Henry studied her with uncertainty.

"I care for you very much, as you know. I respect and honor you. You're a fine man."

His expression didn't change.

"I'm sorry to disappoint you."

Henry quirked his mouth to the side before saying, "But you don't want to marry me."

"It's become a little more complicated than that."

"How so?"

"I truly considered marriage to you, and I didn't find it an unpleasant idea at all. But something just didn't feel quite right about the decision, and I dragged my feet about giving you my answer."

"What happened?"

"I think I know why I didn't say yes." She took a deep breath. "Reverend Hart has asked me to marry him and join his family in Colorado."

Henry's face showed his genuine surprise. He glanced away as if gathering his thoughts and emotions. Without looking back at her, he asked, "You said yes?"

"I said yes."

"And your decision felt right?"

"It did."

He looked at her then, and his gaze was still warm and affectionate. "Of course it did. He's a young man with a bright future. You need someone to look after, and those children couldn't do better than you."

His words brought tears of acute relief to her eyes.

"You and Sam will be making a brand-new start. That's what God does best, you know? Gives second chances."

"Thank you for understanding."

"I told you that you deserved a husband and a family, didn't I? This is it."

Blinking away the moisture in her eyes, Josie knelt at his knees and took his hand. "You're happy for me. You're a good friend."

"You're a good friend, too, Josie. I'm going to miss you."

"You and James will keep each other on your toes."

A smile creased his cheek. He covered the back of her hand with his other one. "I will pray for you without ceasing. And I'll look for letters telling me of the good things you're accomplishing in your new home."

"Thank you. I'm looking forward to a new start. But I have someone else to tell, and to be honest, I'm dreading it."

"Your mother-in-law?"

She nodded. Margaretta would not take the news as graciously as Reverend Martin had. Josie could almost hear the accusations now.

"She *is* quite devoted to your late husband's memory. Margaretta may not understand your need to move on with your life. She's one of those people who lets the past hold them back. She has dwelt on memories of her husband and son until she's probably blown them up into something far greater and better than they truly ever were."

"I feel as though I need to put on my battle armor."

"You're never without it," he answered. "Rest assured the helmet of truth and breastplate of righteousness protect you from those slinging arrows."

"You do know her."

"You might have to accept that she won't give you her blessing. You're not seeking her approval, though, so don't let her discourage you when you know what you're doing is right."

She appreciated his wisdom. "I believe I'm doing what God wants me to."

"God tells us in the book of Jeremiah that he has good plans for our well-being and peace. When you're listening for His direction, you can plan with confidence."

She released his hands and stood. "I'll remember that."

Josie rang the bell on the front door of the house where Bram had grown up. A minute later it opened.

"Josie?" Margaretta blinked with surprise. Josie had never come uninvited. "Well, come in. I'll make tea."

Josie conceded to let her get out her china and make a big fuss out of steeping her imported tea leaves. When eventually they seated themselves on Margaretta's brocade settee, Josie sipped the sweetened brew.

"Do you need something?" Bram's mother asked.

Josie was acutely aware of the woman's intolerance. She'd always been the outsider. But she was leaving, and Margaretta would never influence her life again. The knowledge gave her more confidence. "I've never needed anything but acceptance and perhaps a measure of understanding," she replied. Without giving Margaretta time to form an insult, she pushed on with what she'd come here for. "I'm going to be married again."

The woman gasped. Her face drained of color, and the cup and saucer she held slipped from her hand with a clatter. It landed on the rug without breaking. Tea seeped into the wool fibers.

Josie got up and used her napkin to quickly soak up the liquid.

Ignoring the spill, Margaretta stood. "Of all the ungrateful and mean-spirited things I've ever heard! I guess I could have expected nothing better of you. You'll never be satisfied. Which wealthy man have you dug your claws into this time?"

Sitting back on her heels and looking up, Josie refused to allow the stinging words any credence. "You don't know me at all, if you can think of me like that."

"I know you, and I know your kind. My son's memory means nothing to you."

Josie closed her eyes. She had expected the worst, but Margaretta was the closest thing she had to family, and it didn't feel right to make decisions without letting her know. She couldn't have let her find out from someone else.

"Who is it?" Margaretta asked.

Josie shook her head. "Never mind. I shouldn't have said anything to upset you."

"Of course I'm upset. My only son is dead. I have no grandchildren, only an unappreciative daughter-in-law who can't wait to marry another unsuspecting man."

"Unsuspecting of what?"

"You can be sure that I'll warn this new husband of yours that you're of no use to him in procuring children. If he wants heirs, he'd best look elsewhere. Of course, that suits you, doesn't it? All the money goes into your bank account."

Finding a chink in her armor, those words cut deep into Josie's insecurities and stirred up painful feelings of inadequacy. She released the napkin and cup and stood slowly.

She looked at Bram's mother, unable to comprehend her bitter ire. "He's not rich and he doesn't need children. Reverend Hart actually appreciates me."

"Reverend Hart!" Margaretta shrieked and threw her hands in the air. "You've been with that man every day, likely spending unsupervised hours in his company. I should have suspected you had a plan to ensnare the poor, unsuspecting widower."

Josie shook her head at the hateful accusation. "I had no idea he was even thinking such a thing until last night."

"Last night! And already you've jumped at the chance. How convenient that Reverend Martin is

Get 2 Books FREE!

Steeple Hill Books,
publisher of inspirational fiction,
presents

Love Inspired HISTORICAL

INSPIRATIONAL HISTORICAL ROMANCE

A new series of historical love stories that promise romance, adventure and faith!

FREE BOOKS!   Use the reply card inside to get two free books by outstanding historical romance authors!

FREE GIFTS!   You'll also get two exciting surprise gifts, absolutely free!

GET 2 BOOKS

IF YOU ENJOY A HISTORICAL ROMANCE STORY that reflects solid, traditional values, then you'll like *Love Inspired® Historical* novels. These are engaging tales filled with romance, adventure and faith set in various historical periods from biblical times to World War II.

We'd like to send you two *Love Inspired Historical* novels absolutely free. Accepting them puts you under no obligation to purchase any more books.

HOW TO GET YOUR
2 FREE BOOKS AND TWO FREE GIFTS

1. Return the reply card today, and we'll send you two *Love Inspired Historical* novels, absolutely free! We'll even pay the postage!
2. Accepting free books places you under no obligation to buy anything, ever. The two books have combined cover prices of $11.00 in the U.S. and $13.00 in Canada, but they're yours to keep, free!
3. We hope that after receiving your free books you'll want to remain a subscriber, but the choice is yours–to continue or cancel, any time at all!

EXTRA BONUS

You'll also get two free mystery gifts! (worth about $10)

® and ™ are trademarks owned and used by the trademark owner and/or its licensee.
© 2008 STEEPLE HILL BOOKS.

FREE!

◀ DETACH AND MAIL CARD TODAY! ▶

Return this card promptly to get
2 FREE BOOKS and 2 FREE GIFTS!

Love Inspired
HISTORICAL
INSPIRATIONAL HISTORICAL ROMANCE

YES! Please send me 2 FREE *Love Inspired*
Historical novels, and 2 free mystery gifts as
well. I understand I am under no obligation to
purchase anything, as explained on the back of
this insert.

102 IDL EVLM   302 IDL EVNX

FIRST NAME   LAST NAME

ADDRESS

APT.#   CITY

STATE/PROV.   ZIP/POSTAL CODE

Order online at:
www.LoveInspiredBooks.com

(LIH-2F-09)

Offer limited to one per household and not valid to current subscribers of Love Inspired
Historical books. **Your Privacy -** Steeple Hill Books is committed to protecting your privacy.
Our Privacy Policy is available online at www.SteepleHill.com or upon request from the
Steeple Hill Reader Service. From time to time we make our lists of customers available to
reputable third parties who may have a product or service of interest to you. If you would
prefer for us not to share your name and address, please check here□.

Steeple Hill Reader Service - Here's how it works:

Accepting your 2 free books and 2 free gifts places you under no obligation to buy anything. You may keep the books and gifts and return the shipping statement marked "cancel". If you do not cancel, about a month later we'll send you 4 additional books and bill you just $4.24 each in the U.S. or $4.74 each in Canada. That is a savings of at least 20% off the cover price. It's quite a bargain! Shipping and handling is just 25¢ per book. You may cancel at any time, but if you choose to continue, every other month we'll send you 4 more books, which you may either purchase at the discount price...or return to us and cancel your subscription. *Terms and prices subject to change without notice. Prices do not include applicable taxes. Sales tax applicable in N.Y. Canadian residents will be charged applicable provincial taxes and GST. Offer not valid in Quebec. All orders subject to approval. Credit or debit balances in a customer's account(s) may be offset by any other outstanding balance owed by or to the customer. Books received may not be as shown. Please allow 4 to 6 weeks for delivery. Offer valid while quantities last.

If offer card is missing, write to Steeple Hill Reader Service, 3010 Walden Ave., P.O. Box 1867, Buffalo, NY 14240-1867

BUSINESS REPLY MAIL
FIRST-CLASS MAIL   PERMIT NO. 717   BUFFALO, NY

POSTAGE WILL BE PAID BY ADDRESSEE

Steeple Hill Reader Service
3010 WALDEN AVENUE
PO BOX 1867
BUFFALO NY 14240-9952

NO POSTAGE
NECESSARY
IF MAILED
IN THE
UNITED STATES

back on his feet to pronounce you married before the Hart fellow can get away."

Angry now, Josie picked up her reticule where it lay on a side table. "Well, thank you." She gathered the hem of her skirts in preparation to go. "I'm so glad I came for this little chat. You've been so helpful. I can always count on you when I need a friendly ear or a shoulder to lean on."

She made it as far as the door and turned back. "Your son was *exactly* the same way, God rest his soul."

Margaretta's chest puffed out with indignation, and her face turned beet-red. "How *dare* you speak to me that way?"

With her head held high, Josie spun and kept walking through the foyer, out the front door, down the steps. She would never, *never* have another word to say to that woman as long as she lived. Margaretta may be lonely and bereaved, but she'd been just plain mean to start with.

"Josie!" Margaretta called. "Don't you dare turn your back on me!"

Josie wasn't accountable to Bram's mother for anything. Reverend Martin had counseled her not to seek the woman's approval, and Josie hadn't expected it. She had endured all she intended to. That chapter of her life was behind her.

"Josie!"

And getting farther behind all the time.

She actually smiled and slowed her walk to a stroll.

* * *

That evening was Reverend Martin's Bible study, in which Josie and the Harts participated, and the following day was full for Sam, so it wasn't until Thursday that he was able to gather Josie and the three girls for their meeting.

He asked all of them to join him for a midday picnic.

Abigail and Anna thought it was great fun. They gathered purple clover and made chains for their hair and to wear as necklaces. Anna made one for Josie and hung it around her neck. Elisabeth had brought along a book, and she sat cross-legged under a tree, reading.

Josie had packed sandwiches and apples, along with pint jars of lemonade. After they ate, Sam called the girls and asked them to gather on the faded blanket in the shade.

"Josie and I have something to share with you," he said.

"We're getting a lamb!" Anna squealed.

"We can't take a lamb all the way to Colorado with us," Sam explained.

Elisabeth gave her youngest sister an I-told-you-so look and turned her attention back to her father.

Sam didn't beat around the bush or preface the news. "Josie and I are going to be married."

Chapter Ten

Sam's daughters stared at him.

"She's coming with us the rest of the way, and she'll live with us in our new home."

"Mrs. Randolph is going to be your wife now?" Anna asked.

"You'll have to get used to calling me Josie."

"But what about Mama?" Elisabeth asked, her voice revealing her shock and concern.

"What about her, Elisabeth?" Sam asked.

"How can you just forget about her and marry Mrs. Randolph?"

"I haven't forgotten your mother," Sam answered. "I'll never forget her. I loved her very much."

Elisabeth's chin quivered. "But you're getting married again."

"That doesn't mean I didn't love your mother. It only means we're making a new family."

"I *like* Josie," Anna said. "I'm glad she's coming with us."

Abigail gave Josie a shy smile, but glanced at Elisabeth and said nothing.

"Josie wanted a baby," Anna blurted out, "but she didn't get one. Can we give her a baby? Can it be our brother?"

Her question hung in the air for an uncomfortable moment.

Afraid of what Sam's expression would reveal, Josie couldn't look at him, so she didn't see his initial reaction. Her heart raced in the silence.

Apparently, he finally gathered his wits. "We'll just wait and see what God has in store for us."

A sinking sensation dropped in Josie's belly. She'd been so caught up in the anticipation that this particular reality hadn't entered her head. She couldn't have children. What if Sam wanted more? She would have to tell him. He might change his mind!

Enthusiasm drained from her spirit in a downward rush. What had she been thinking? Announcing an impending marriage might have been for naught.

Elisabeth's blue eyes held a cold accusation. The girl touched the bodice of her dress where Josie knew she wore her mother's wedding ring on a slender cord. Josie understood. Elisabeth obviously felt her father was betraying her mother's memory.

She regretted the parallel she drew to Margaretta's narrow-mindedness. This was nothing like that. Elisabeth's was a fresh loss, and she probably saw Josie as a threat to her importance with her father.

Sam spoke of the trip they'd soon be taking and the preparations necessary.

"How many rivers are there, Papa?" Anna asked.

"The only big one is the Platte." The fact that he knew and answered immediately proved it was a serious issue he'd already considered. We'll cross at Ogallala, where a ferry will take us across."

Josie didn't know about the exact location of their destination, but Union Pacific had completed laying rail across Nebraska two years ago. She would ask Sam about that when they were alone. Perhaps a train wouldn't be as terrifying to the girls as their wagon.

After more discussion, Abigail and Anna chased a butterfly across the grass and Elisabeth went back to her book. The fact that she didn't look at Josie again plainly told of her distress.

Josie gathered her courage. "There's something I didn't mention. It might make a difference."

Sam plucked a long blade of grass and held it between his teeth. "What is it?"

"You know I was married for several years."

"Yes."

"I never had any children. I'm barren."

Sam blinked and took the grass from his mouth. "I'm sorry, Josie."

She didn't want to hear his answer, but, steeling herself, she asked anyway. "Does that make a difference? I'll understand if you change your mind."

Her heart raced as she waited.

"Of course it doesn't change my mind. I already have children. I don't need any more. When I said I was sorry, I meant I felt badly for you if you were disappointed."

Relief flooded over her in a wave. Tears prickled behind her lids, but she blinked them back and looked away with a single nod. "Good. Good, then."

"You'll have your hands full with the girls," he assured her.

"I will at that." She remembered the other subject. "Sam. I'm not questioning your wisdom or decisions when I ask out of curiosity why you haven't considered taking the train to Colorado. The railroad would be much quicker, and perhaps safer."

"It would also be far costlier," he explained. "We have a wagon load of belongings, plus our passage. Carrie and I made the decision to take our belongings, even though the trip was more difficult. It meant a lot to her to have her things." A muscle in his jaw worked. "Another poor choice, since it ended up costing her life."

"You had no way of knowing. You did what you believed was the right thing. We could all torture ourselves with regrets if we didn't move past them. What about now? From here to Colorado?"

"I'd have to sell everything left for the tickets. I don't know if the girls could cope with that. They need something of their former life when we get there."

"I intend to ship my things," she said. "Not everything, of course, but some of my furniture and of course the clothing I don't pack for travel. It couldn't be that much more to add your things to mine."

He studied her. "You're willing to suffer the cost of shipping your belongings?"

"I'm selling my house. I can afford it."

"You don't owe anything for your home?"

"Bram paid for it when we were married. And as his widow, everything that was his became mine."

"I think you're underestimating the cost of including our things."

"I don't mind. I want to do it to make the journey easier. And safer."

His rusty brown gaze turned to the countryside while he thought. "*You* would feel safer?"

"Much. And it would be so much easier on the girls."

He turned his gaze back to her. "I could sell the wagon and then buy another to finish the last leg of the trip. There are no rails leading to Jackson Springs."

She agreed with a smile.

"But if the cost is extreme you'll let me know, so I can figure out a way to help."

"It won't be. Can we tell them?"

"Let's tell them."

The news of their engagement buzzed through Durham faster than a swarm of bees. Josie was elated by the greetings and congratulations she heard at church and in the mercantile that week. It did her heart good to know that Margaretta's narrow-minded opinion was hers alone, and that Josie's friends and acquaintances were happy for her.

For the next few weeks, Margaretta didn't speak to her at church, nor did she request Josie's presence when she made her trek to the graveyard.

On the Sunday before the week of their wedding, Sam noticed Margaretta standing alone inside the picket fence. "I understand people's reluctance to let their loved ones go. It's a blessing she has a place to come to, to remember her son, but she's perhaps too zealous in clinging to the past."

Josie hadn't told him how rude the woman had been to her. She simply nodded.

"She came to see me, you know."

Josie glanced up at him in surprise. Margaretta had threatened she would warn him about her. "I doubt that was pleasant for you."

"I don't think I was able to set her mind at ease."

"I doubt anyone could."

"According to her, you're the devil incarnate."

"Something like that."

"She believes you're using me for your own selfish purposes."

Josie got a sinking feeling in her stomach. It was one thing for Bram's mother to have such a distorted opinion of her, but pressing those beliefs onto others carried the venom too far. Had she put questions in Sam's head? Doubts?

Sam looked at Josie directly. "I told her if you wanted a wealthy man, you'd made a poor choice."

Of course one bitter woman's prattling hadn't changed his mind. He was a man of wisdom and integrity. She smiled in relief. "Is that why your sermon this morning was about not setting up our treasures here on earth?"

"It's a good reminder for everyone." He glanced toward the front of the church, where Reverend Martin sat on a white bench, greeting parishioners. This was his first Sunday to make the trek from the parsonage and attend the morning service.

"He looks tired," Sam said.

"He can rest after we eat. I'd best go see to the meal, while you help him back to the house."

Their last Sunday dinner in Durham was pleasant. James came by and ate with them. Reverend Martin brought up the approaching wedding. Ever since Josie had actually realized he would be performing the nuptials, she had appreciated him all the more. He was truly happy for her. The man was a living example of unselfish love.

James and Elisabeth played checkers afterward, and then moved out of doors, where they sat on the grass in the shade.

"I don't want her to grow up," Sam said from where he stood at the window in Henry's study.

"She's only thirteen," Josie reminded him.

"She's mature for her age."

"She has a level head."

"She's always been serious and thoughtful," he said.

"Has she always wanted to go everywhere with you?"

Sam seemed thoughtful for a moment. Josie knew that Elisabeth was most often the one who traveled with him, and she always questioned him about his visits. "She has."

"She wants your approval. She works hard to please you."

"She's the oldest, so that's natural."

Josie considered her next words. "Abigail wants to go places with you, too, but if Elisabeth is going, she holds her tongue."

He turned to look at her. "Abigail has never expressed an interest in accompanying me."

Josie suspected Abigail's hesitation might be because she feared being looked over for her sister. "She may not want to compete for your attention or affection."

"My relationship with each of my daughters is different."

Josie agreed with a nod. It wasn't her place to question how he handled things with his children. She changed the subject. "Only a few more days, and we'll be married and leaving," she said. "The time has passed quickly."

"The time we've been here has been well-spent," he said. "Henry thinks I was here to help him, but it was the other way around."

"I have no doubt that God brought you to Durham for a reason," she replied. "Because He loves us, and He's watching out for us. When we put our trust in Him, He can do things we never thought possible."

"Like moving away from your home?" Sam asked.

"Moving away isn't all that difficult."

"I pray you'll still be able to say that in a few weeks, when you're faced with a new city and the responsibility of three daughters."

She was tired of sitting on the edge of life, watching other people have families. She was grabbing on to this opportunity for all she was worth. "Just hearing you say I'll have three daughters makes me happy, Sam."

He'd said nothing of the fact that she would also have a new husband. Josie couldn't help studying him at the window and thinking of all that would entail.

She wouldn't be alone any longer.

Sometimes, when she heard the way Anna or Abigail spoke of their mother, and saw the look on Sam's face, she remembered she wasn't his first choice, or the woman he loved with all his heart. He'd lost that woman, and Josie didn't hope to replace her. Nor would she try.

But she longed for the comfort and intimacy of a family. She would see to their needs and make herself indispensable. She would make Samuel Hart a good wife. Doing her very best and earning his approval would be enough for her.

* * *

Anticipation hummed through the congregation seated in the small wooden church. Josie held the bouquet of daisies James had thoughtfully picked for her, and tried not to crush the stems and stain her white gloves.

"Are you ready for this?" Henry asked her with a smile.

They stood at the front of the church. The noon sunlight shone through the tall, narrow windows, creating long arrows of light across the worn oak floors.

"I'm ready," she answered confidently.

Josie hadn't seen Reverend Martin in his suit for months. He'd lost weight, so the black coat didn't quite fit his frame the way it once had.

A couple of years ago she'd given away the satin dress she'd worn to marry Bram. This time she'd chosen a pastel yellow confection from the dress-maker and had lace inserted around the collar and cuffs.

She wore a strand of pearls and matching earbobs that had belonged to her mother and had donned the wispy hat the girls helped her make, with tiny paper roses and Battenburg lace—not a veil, because that would have been inappropriate for her second wedding.

She was more than ready for this day and every-thing it brought.

Sam entered the church from the side door and

caught sight of Josie. She turned, and a jolt of surprise shot through him. She was beautiful! Sunlight illuminated her pale yellow dress. A tiny lace hat showed off her lustrous dark hair. Thick lashes fringed her lovely eyes, and her smile was as warm and welcoming as the woman herself.

He'd made this arrangement for purely practical reasons, but he was taking a lovely young woman as his wife. He glanced to where Elisabeth, Abigail and Anna sat on the front bench in their best Sunday dresses, their shining pale hair braided. Anna beamed from ear to ear. Abigail gave him a hesitant smile. Elisabeth refused to look up and meet his eyes.

She would come around.

Sam felt good about marrying Josie. Even the day and the weather were perfect. This marriage was the best choice he'd made in a long time. He looked at Henry and nodded.

Reverend Martin performed the ceremony, reading from the book of Corinthians and encouraging them to keep God at the center of their marriage.

"And now, by the power given to me by God and the state of Nebraska, I pronounce you Mr. and Mrs. Samuel Hart."

Josie had anticipated the words, but they still gave her a tingle of pleasure. Sam's hand was large and warm as it enveloped hers.

"You may kiss the bride."

She looked up. Sam's expression didn't reveal his

thoughts. He had never kissed her. Without hesitation, he leaned forward and pressed a kiss to the corner of her lips—sort of a half kiss, half peck on the cheek that, however unsatisfactory, sealed their vows.

They were man and wife. Her new life had begun.

She smiled hesitantly and together they turned to face the approving congregation. Anna, a vision in the pale dress that nearly matched the color of Josie's, ran forward to hug her father around the waist. She released him and gave Josie an affectionate hug, pressing her head into Josie's midriff and squeezing her tightly.

Josie touched Anna's hair and thanked God for the child's loving, accepting nature.

Ten minutes later Sam held a signed certificate. The women of the church had prepared cake, punch and coffee, and now served them in the shaded side yard. Josie glanced at the simple gold band on her finger. She'd had so many dreams and expectations of her first husband and their marriage, and most of them had been unrealistic. She wouldn't make the same mistake this time. She would be satisfied and therefore not disappointed.

She accepted the hugs and well-wishes of her friends and neighbors. Margaretta was conspicuously absent, and Pauline Wilber mentioned the fact, as a small gathering crowded around Josie.

"She should have married again herself," Nettie said. "Maybe she wouldn't be so miserable if she had."

"You're so good for putting up with her all these years," Laura Caldwell added. "You deserve this new start."

Josie thanked them and changed the subject.

She had asked the invited guests not to bring gifts. Most of her belongings had already been sold, donated or shipped to Colorado, along with Sam's furniture and trunks. Anything extra would make their trip more difficult.

To her delight, a couple that had just added a new baby to their family bought Josie's house. Josie had spent the last two nights with Nettie Boardman.

In winding up her life here, she had signed an agreement with Frank Carlisle. He would be sending her a payment every month to pay for the other half of the newspaper. She looked forward to that as an additional income that would help the family.

There were a few gifts, so they opened embroidered dish towels and monogrammed handkerchiefs and thanked the givers.

Tomorrow morning they would set out for their new home.

Sam and the girls delivered her to Nettie's, so she could change and collect her things. They returned to the parsonage, where they spent their evening as usual.

Once it grew late, Sam tucked the girls into bed.

Josie packed the gifts and readied their satchels for morning. After changing, she brushed out her hair and glanced around the room. She didn't know what

to expect from now on. Sam had kissed her, only
when pressed in front of their wedding guests. He
didn't have those kinds of feelings for her. But it was
okay.

Josie put her hairbrush back in her satchel and
removed her Bible. She had a lifetime ahead. She
was well pleased with her new life.

Chapter Eleven

Their travel through Nebraska was fairly quick, as the train chugged across open stretches of prairie. Anna and Abigail were fascinated with every aspect of the trip, from the passengers who accompanied them to the scenery.

Josie, who had traveled before and knew the hardships, had purchased tickets for six seats, even though there were only five of them. The additional seat gave them two poorly padded benches that faced each other and a little room for wiggle. They took turns using the extra seat for uncomfortable naps, during which Sam filled the space between benches opposite each other with a crate.

Toward evening the first day, a man ahead of them spotted a herd of bison and alerted the passengers. The Hart family watched with fascination as the beasts grazed beneath the orange sphere of the sun.

Travel became slower as they reached Colorado, with its winding curves and steady inclines. The train stopped at every station to take on water and coal. The travelers were afforded anywhere from thirty to sixty minutes to use the primitive facilities and, if they were fortunate, buy a meal and a drink.

The inside of the railcar was hot and stuffy. Even though dust and smoke blew in the open windows, the ventilation was necessary.

A young woman traveling alone with an infant occupied a seat behind them. The child fussed and cried, much to the dismay of the poor girl and the disapproval of the other passengers.

"I haven't seen her eat," Sam said quietly to Josie, late the second morning of their journey.

Uncertain of his meaning, she glanced from Elisabeth, who was reading, to Anna and Abigail, working on quilt squares. They'd all had breakfast that morning. "Who?"

"The girl behind us. I'm thinking she has no money."

The child's fussing again drew scowls from nearby passengers. "What can we do?" Josie asked.

"Invite her to join us when we stop next."

"All right."

Deborah Bowers declined Josie's first offer to join them, so Josie offered to hold the child while the girl used the facility. Upon her return, Deborah thought better of her answer and accompanied them into the rustic dining hall attached to the station.

Josie held the tired little boy throughout their meal. She fed Jack a few bites of bread she soaked in milk, and he ate them happily.

"He's a good little fellow," Deborah told them. "He's not used to being held so much. My husband has a place ready for us in Fort Collins. We've already been traveling for a week."

"We're going as far as Fort Collins," Sam told her. "Why don't you let my wife and I help you with him?"

Hearing Sam call her his wife pleased Josie so much she got tears in her eyes.

"You're so kind," Deborah said with heartfelt gratitude. "Everyone else is giving me dirty looks."

"If you think he'd sleep for a while, we have an extra seat for that purpose," Josie offered. "We can cushion the crate with his blankets and let him nap."

Deborah tried to pay for her meal, but Sam used his own coins. They boarded the train and he temporarily took Deborah's seat so she could get Jack to sleep and sit beside him.

"Your husband is a kind man," Deborah said to Josie later. The girls were all napping while sitting up and Jack was sound asleep.

"Yes," Josie replied with a smile. "He is."

"I hope my husband still looks at me the way your husband looks at you after we've been married as long as you have."

Deborah's statement took Josie by surprise. How did Sam look at her? As she ruminated that question,

Deborah's misconception became clear. "We've only just been married actually. I'm the girls' stepmother."

"That makes their blond hair clear to me," Deborah said with a nod. "And the fact that you're newlyweds explains those admiring glances."

Josie's cheeks grew warm, and it had nothing to do with the heat inside the car.

When the two returned to their own seats later, Josie tried to catch Sam looking at her, but she didn't notice anything out of the ordinary.

"How much longer?" Abigail asked after a supper of tough steaks and nearly burnt corn bread.

"This is the last night we'll spend on the train," Sam assured her. "Tomorrow we'll reach Fort Collins and buy a wagon and horses for the rest of the trip."

"And then we'll take the wagon to our new house and unpack our stuff," Anna supplied.

"Wait till you see Mama's teapot and cups," Abigail told Josie. "They have violets painted on them."

"I'm sure they're lovely," Josie answered.

"We won't have everything all at once," Sam told them. "Josie shipped a lot of things ahead by rail. We'll bring some of them from Fort Collins to Jackson Springs, but the rest will be delivered in due time."

"What about beds?" Abigail asked. "Will we have beds?"

"We brought one with us," Sam reminded her.

"I had one shipped," Josie added. "We'll buy another when we get in our home."

"Perhaps not right away," Sam told her. "The girls can make do with pallets or sleep together."

Any bed sounded good to Josie right about then. She was exhausted. Her back and hips hurt from the uncomfortable seats and lack of exercise. The girls fell silent and eventually nodded off to sleep, with Anna on the makeshift portion. Josie shifted to find the least torturous position and closed her eyes.

She had drifted off when behind her Jack fussed. Josie got up, reached across a snoring lady to reach Deborah and took Jack. She settled with him on her lap and gave him the brass compact from her reticule to hold. He chewed on the side and looked up at her in the semidarkness.

Sam studied Josie from beneath the lowered brim of his hat. She was as hot and uncomfortable as everyone else, but she made the best of every situation and didn't complain. Her face had been flushed a becoming shade of pink nearly the entire journey, and the dampness and humidity had coaxed wispy corkscrew curls to frame her cheeks and temples.

He couldn't forget the sight of her in her lemony-colored wedding dress, nor could he ignore the anticipation that had coursed through him when Reverend Martin and instructed him to kiss her, and he'd done so.

He hadn't married her for his own gain or pleasure. He'd married her for his daughters, and he believed Carrie would have approved. But what would Carrie have thought of his reaction to that kiss? He'd immediately been ashamed that he could so easily have abandoned thoughts of his wife and entertained the promise of new possibilities.

Lord, thank You for strength and wisdom, he prayed.

Josie was so good with the girls. And apparently she would have been excellent at comforting and mothering an infant. Sam never questioned God about why things were the way they were, but he did believe it was a shame that Josie had been unable to have her own babies.

But God knew everything that was and would be, so He'd known in advance that Sam's children would need the perfect mother at just this place in time.

Soon they'd be in their new home. Living together as man and wife. *Lord, thank You for strength and wisdom.*

Sam closed his eyes and slept.

This time his dreams were not about his wife's death.

He dreamed of a woman with dark, wavy hair that escaped the pins and curled about her face. He admired her caramel eyes and dewy pink skin. In his dream he kissed her.

And he wasn't sorry.

"Four days of dust and heat without a bed or a bath makes me admire trail drivers and soldiers all the more." Josie brushed at her hopelessly wrinkled skirt, then shook the hem.

Sam loaded the last of the foodstuffs into the back of their wagon and tied them down on top of the heavy items. "We sometimes went weeks without a bath on our way from Philadelphia."

She wrinkled her nose. She had purchased supplies for the trip while he secured a wagon and team, and they now stood in the street outside the mercantile, ready to travel.

"How many days will we travel in the wagon, Father?" Elisabeth asked from her position beside the rear wheel.

"Three or four, depending on the team and how often we stop." He fastened the canvas over the back opening to keep out as much dust as possible.

Abigail remained on the boardwalk in the shade. Her bonnet had lost its starch in the heat and humidity, and the brim sagged over one eye. "It will be scary without other wagons."

"It's a well-traveled route, Ab," her father assured her. "We'll likely see other travelers coming and going. And there's a stage, so we'll pass a way station."

"And no rivers, Papa."

"No rivers," he assured Anna.

She gave him a nod, and her eyes widened with enthusiasm for her next subject. "Did you see the big kitty beside the barrel?"

"I did," Sam answered. He reached for her on the boardwalk, lifted her to kiss her cheek and effortlessly swooped her up to the front of the wagon.

"He rubbed hisself on my boots an' let me pet him," she said. "He's more friendlier than Reverend Martin's kitty."

"Cats are rather like people in that regard," he answered. "Some are friendly, others are not."

Sam found an empty crate and positioned it so Abigail and Elisabeth could climb up. They ducked inside the wagon, seating themselves on the interior bench.

Anna remained standing so she could ask, "Are lambs friendly?"

"Some are," he answered, looking at Josie and raising his eyebrows as if to say, *She isn't letting that go, is she?* Instead, he asked, "Ready?"

Josie walked to the front and used the crate, then the spokes of the front wheel as a ladder. Sam helped her the rest of the way.

Anna scurried to the seat just inside the cover of the canvas, and Josie situated herself on the hard seat.

Sam tucked the crate between them on the floor, but instead of sitting, he reached for Josie's hand. At the touch, she glanced up in surprise. He urged her to stand and turn, then led her under the canvas arch. Crouching in the space before his daughters, he took Elisabeth's hand with his free one.

Anna and Abigail clutched hands and Abigail reached for Josie so they formed a circle. Josie's heart fluttered at being part of this family. Sam's hand was large and strong and Abigail's small and soft.

"Thank You, Lord, for a prosperous journey by Your will. We commit our way to You," he prayed, and emotion welled inside Josie.

"Father, I pray for the people of Jackson Springs, that their spirits are open to whatever gift and whatever Word it is You'd have me impart to them. Lord, make me an encourager for them. Open doors for Elisabeth and Abigail and Anna, so that they will have friends and teachers to bless them. Father, as my wife, I thank You that Josie is taking her own special gift to your children there. Bless the labor of her hands and the desires of her heart, as she prepares our home and opens it to the people.

"Now keep us safe in all our ways as we travel, and we praise You in the mighty name of Jesus."

"Amen," Josie and the girls chorused.

As Sam seated himself, picked up the reins and clucked to the horses, Josie was filled to overflowing with gratitude for this good, upright man God had brought into her life.

If she'd set out to search a hundred cities and a thousand places, she would never have found a man seeking God's heart as determinedly as this one beside her now.

And he had chosen to marry her.

Thank You, thank You, thank You.

Sam, Elisabeth and Abigail were familiar with setting up a camp, gathering firewood and finding water, if need be, but everything was new to Josie.

She burned the first night's biscuits and undercooked them the second night. On the third evening, Sam took over and made the biscuits over the fire, while Josie used another skillet to fry the two whitefish he and Elisabeth had caught in a nearby stream.

At least she'd been assured that this was their last night before reaching Jackson Springs. Each night, she and the girls had slept on top of the furniture and supplies lying in the bed of the wagon, padded with blankets, while Sam slept on the ground underneath.

"The evenings are so much cooler than the days here," she said. "I'm going to like that for sleeping."

"I'm keeping a journal of all the trees and flowers and animals," Abigail told them. "I don't know what all of them are called, but my teacher might be able to help me."

"I found a pretty stone while I was gathering sticks," Elisabeth said.

She didn't often add to the conversation, so Josie stopped eating to ask about her discovery. Even though the conditions were less than ideal, their trip had been a good experience. The close confines had given them opportunities to talk.

"There's a secluded spot just beyond those cottonwoods," Sam told them, indicating the area. "It's a perfect opportunity to bathe and wash any clothes you might want freshened."

No one wanted to miss the luxury of being clean when they arrived in town the next day, so the females took turns bathing. They gathered around the campfire, drying their hair while Sam bathed and tended the horses.

He tucked his daughters into the wagon for the night and returned. "The church has a parsonage for us," Sam told her. She had washed the plates in the stream and packed away all but the coffeepot. They would eat the remaining biscuits in the morning. "The council mentioned that there was an allowance if we prefer different housing, but I'm sure it will be sufficient."

Josie imagined a home as comfortable as Reverend Martin's and nodded. She poured each of them a cup of coffee and sat on an empty crate near Sam. "I'm sorry I haven't been more of a help out here."

"You haven't complained a bit, and for that I'm thankful."

"I'm having an adventure," she said. "I've never seen the mountains, and as they become bigger and bigger on the horizon, the sight takes my breath away. Everything is green and lush, and there are so many trees."

"The countryside is beautiful," Sam agreed, but he was looking at her where she sat, with her hair loose over her shoulders.

Josie glanced aside. Was that the look Deborah had mentioned? "I'd better get ready for bed."

She stood and made her way into the brush that surrounded their campsite. On her return, something rubbed against the hem of her skirts, nearly tripping her. A startled shriek escaped before she could tell herself it was probably only one of the muskrats or martens Sam had told them about.

With her heart racing, she shot toward the safety of the fire. Sam dashed forward to meet her halfway. "What is it?"

"Something in the brush surprised me, is all." She felt foolish, but she was glad for the arm he wrapped around her, and she tucked into his embrace with a rush of relief.

They stood that way, out of the circle of firelight, with the moon bathing them in its glow.

Sam smelled of the soap he'd used, along with the same touch of wood smoke that clung to all of them. He was warm and solid, and a sense of security and well-being infused her. Josie hadn't been held this way for a long time.

"I feel safe here," she said softly.

She felt his hand in her hair, threading through the length like a caress, coming to rest on her shoulder.

Her heart beat faster than it had when she'd been startled moments ago. After a second's hesitation, she looked up.

Sam met her gaze in the darkness. She couldn't see his eyes. Could he see the moon reflected in hers?

He moved his hand from her shoulder to cup her jaw with his palm. His thumb moved along her cheekbone in a gentle caress. The night sounds closed around them, cushioning them in the mysterious cocoon of the night.

Chapter Twelve

Without conscious thought or effort, she found herself locked in his embrace. He lowered his head and she met his kiss with eager anticipation.

The rightness of the moment took over.

He was a mystery, this husband, strong and tender at the same time. She'd been more than ready to cast aside loneliness and entrust herself to him and the future she believed waited for them. The future seemed painted with exquisite possibilities.

He represented everything that was good and perfect about fathers and husbands. Strange, unfamiliar feelings made her light-headed. She couldn't help the little sigh that escaped her.

Josie had no idea there were kisses like this.

Kissing him was everything she'd ever imagined it could be, and she wanted to cry with the rightness of the moment.

Sam ended the kiss and rested his forehead on hers. She recognized her keen disappointment that the moment had ended.

He threaded his fingers into her hair. She reached up to skim his jaw with her fingertips.

Sam reacted to her touch with a start, releasing her. Though he kept a hand on her elbow to steady her, he took a step back, putting distance between them. "It's late," was all he said.

Josie tried to make sense of his rapid change and his obvious discomfort. "Yes, of course."

She thought she'd replied, but wasn't sure the words had actually passed her lips.

He removed his hand from her arm and turned toward the fire.

Josie followed at a slower pace.

He regretted kissing her.

A debilitating ache knotted in her chest and swelled to crowd the newfound joy from her heart.

Had he been reminded of his beloved Carrie? Undoubtedly. Their evening around the fire most likely stirred up memories of their trip to Nebraska. Maybe kissing Josie was a disappointment.

She got angry with herself then. She'd vowed a hundred times that she wouldn't allow her expectations to swell out of proportion. Idealism only set her up for a fall, as she well knew.

While he banked the fire, she climbed the wagon wheel and silently made her way to where the girls slept soundly. After removing her outer clothing, she found her spot. The space was crowded with four of them, but the squeeze was better than lying out of doors and most likely encountering insects and scurrying creatures.

I am content, she told God silently. *You provide all my needs, and my soul is satisfied.* Her distress was childish, and she refused to let foolish emotions control her and steal her joy. She was delighted to be here, grateful to be starting a new life.

If she gave herself over to the growing urge to cry, she would wake the girls, so she closed her eyes against the dark and prayed.

The following morning, Sam led the horses to their positions and fastened the tongue to their harnesses. By the time he had them ready, Josie had coffee made and now divided the biscuits. She handed each of them an apple, avoiding Sam's eyes and careful not to graze his hand with her fingers. He found himself studying her for a reaction to his presence.

Last night he'd lain awake far too long for a man who needed to be alert for the day's travel. His feelings toward this woman were confusing, and he didn't like his weakness one bit. His obligation was to his family's safety, and he had no business allowing an attraction to Josie to distract him.

He was responsible for all of them. A woman's influence never aided a logical decision, and he needed to make choices for their safety. He'd married her to take care of the girls. He hadn't expected to be so absorbed with thoughts of her…and he hadn't expected to think about the curve of her cheek or the way she smiled.

"Do you want to sit beside your father this morning?" Josie asked Anna.

"Oh yes, thank you!" the child replied.

"We'll take turns today, so you can each see your new home a little better."

Was Josie avoiding him? The thought and the possibility disturbed him more than they should have.

Eventually, the road took them past sprawling ranches with horses and cattle on the hillsides and houses tucked into the valleys. When the sun was high overhead, he led the team across a field to the shade of a stand of willows, with drooping branches and crooked, reddish trunks.

While Josie got out the makings for sliced ham and bread, he dipped water from their barrel and made several trips to the horses. The mundane task allowed him to watch her from beneath the brim of his hat. Everything she did was graceful; her voice, when she spoke to the girls, was gentle, her words kind. He'd made a good decision.

After they ate, Anna inspected a thicket of chokecherries and brought a handful to show Josie. "Can we eat 'em?"

Josie nodded. "While we're here, let's fill a pail and we'll make jelly when we get to our new house."

A little over an hour later, from her seat beside her father, Abigail spotted the town. "There it is! Is that it, Papa?"

"That's it."

Josie, Elisabeth and Anna crowded behind the front seat to get their first glimpse of Jackson Springs. Josie's initial reaction was to marvel at the way the various-colored buildings stood on slopes of uneven heights. She was used to the flat plains of the prairie, not the wooded inclines or ore-stained escarpments that sectioned this town into levels.

"It's charming!" she said with delight.

"There's the church!" Abigail cried, pointing toward a white steeple rising against the startlingly blue, cloudless sky.

"Thank You for safe travel and for blessing us with all we need for our new life," Sam said in a husky voice.

Tears blurred Josie's vision.

He chose that moment to glance over his shoulder, and directly into her eyes. They shared a silent moment of expectation and excitement. The side of his mouth turned up in an uncustomary grin.

She blinked away tears and turned her attention back to the town.

"Let's go see the church." Sam clucked to the horses and shook the reins.

Main Street had most likely been the very center of town at one time, but homes and businesses now sprawled along inclines to the west and south. The buildings on the thoroughfare were all the same height and constructed of brick, though their facades were trimmed with bright blues and reds, and the top of each made a unique silhouette against the sky.

The general store bore a shingled porch roof, and two gingerbread-trimmed windows with canvas awnings that looked like lidded eyes in the upper story. A portly fellow in a white apron paused his sweeping to raise a hand.

"Welcome to Jackson Springs!"

"Who-oa," Sam called and tugged the team to a halt. "Afternoon, sir."

"What's your business?" the man asked.

"I'm Reverend Hart," Sam replied. "This is my wife, Josie, and these are my daughters."

Two women who'd come out of a nearby building stepped to the edge of the boardwalk. "We've been expectin' you," the lady in a blue calico dress said with a smile.

"The parsonage is the white house beside the church," the other woman told them. "The ladies have stocked the pantry with enough to see you through a few days while you settle in. And now that we know you're here, we'll bring supper tonight."

"That's exceptionally kind of you," Sam replied and Josie nodded.

After a few more pleasantries, Sam guided the horses and turned onto Birch Street, where the church sat.

The wagon rolled to a stop before the only house right beside the handsome house of worship.

Josie stared. Had there been some mistake? Hadn't they been expecting a *family?*

Sam collected himself and looped the reins around the cleat. In the next instant, he hopped down from the seat to the ground, then turned and helped the girls, one after the other. When Josie stood above him, he reached for her.

Their eyes met and she recalled his prayer, giving thanks for all he needed to start over. Did his thanks include her?

His strong hands were warm at her waist, and she covered them with her own. The moment seemed to stretch out until they were absorbed in each other's eyes. She was his wife now. They'd arrived at their new home, and this was a fresh beginning for all of them.

She hopped down, and he settled her lightly on the ground. As though he didn't want to release her, one hand remained at the small of her back while he turned and studied the arrangement of the church and parsonage on the same parcel of land. There was probably only ten yards between the two structures.

The little house had been given a fresh coat of paint, and it was unembellished, without a shutter or a flower or even a porch. She stepped ahead of him finally, to climb the four steps leading to the door. The portal opened directly into a tiny little room with a braided rug. Josie's bright mood dimmed.

Another door opened into a bedroom that would hold one bed and little else.

The kitchen sat beside the first room. It held a narrow stove and a cupboard. Right beside the kitchen was the only other bedroom, marginally bigger than the first, though the extra feet were in length, not width.

"There's no closet," Elisabeth pointed out.

"And no dining room," Abigail added.

"Will all three of us sleep in this room?" Elisabeth asked, her eyes wide with dismay.

And probably in the same bed, Josie figured. There wasn't room for two.

"We've done just fine till now," Sam said. "How much room do we need? As soon as we're settled, you'll be at school all day long. I can work at the church during the day. It looks plenty big enough to have an extra room for my desk and books."

The girls said nothing, but the excitement that they'd all shared at seeing the town and anticipating their new home had drained away.

Josie had never seen such a tiny house.

Chapter Thirteen

"Where do we bathe?" Elisabeth asked.

Through the window, Josie spotted a structure that obviously wasn't the outhouse because it had a chimney. She opened the back door, and the others followed her out.

A stack of firewood had been neatly piled within a wooden lean-to. The little building, no bigger than a shed, but sided and roofed just like the house, held laundry tubs, buckets, a copper bathing tub and an ancient cast-iron stove.

"Here you go," Sam told them. "A place for canning, cooking, laundry and bathing."

Elisabeth cast a skeptical glance around the room. "Doesn't it get awfully cold in the mountains in the winter?"

"I'm assured it does," he replied.

Josie silently agreed it would be inconvenient to

run between the two buildings to bathe, but it was a small hardship.

"Paul wrote the book of Philippians while he was in jail," Sam reminded them. "In a dungeon. And what did he talk about? Joy, that's what. 'Rejoice in the Lord always, and again I say rejoice.' He had joy in spite of his circumstances, and his circumstances were a lot worse than these."

He headed for the door. "After I have a look at the church, I'll bring in as much as I can unload on my own. The bureau and bed will have to wait for more hands."

"I'll help, Papa!" Anna called, running after him.

The three females stood in the silence of the little outbuilding. Elisabeth and Abigail looked at each other and then at Josie. "It's dreadful, don't you agree?" Elisabeth asked.

Josie chose her words carefully. Their father had hidden his own disappointment well and had been adamant about being joyful. "I am quite surprised at how small it is, yes. Perhaps the last preacher was unmarried or his children were grown and gone."

She headed back toward the house and the girls trailed behind her.

In her mind, she was picturing all the furniture and belongings that would be arriving soon. Would they have to sell everything after all? Would they have to find storage?

All her dreams for making a grand, comfortable home, and entertaining the parishioners, and holding

Bible studies and quilting circles were perched to fly out the window.

The five of them would be hard-pressed to sit comfortably in that small parlor—or in this kitchen, for that matter.

She opened the single cupboard to find canned meat and vegetables, flour, sugar and coffee. "That was nice of them."

"I wish we'd never left Philadelphia," Elisabeth said from behind her.

Josie turned and caught the disappointment and frustration in her expression.

"If we'd stayed there, none of this would be happening. Mama would still be alive, and we'd still have our rooms and our beds and our friends. This is a dreadful house in a dreadful town, and I don't want to be here."

She turned and ran out the back door.

Josie knew better than to imagine she could comfort her. She stared at the open doorway. She understood Elisabeth's disillusionment.

"Everything looks quite clean," she said to Abigail. "Let's go ahead and bring in a few things."

Two young men arrived to help Sam carry in the trunks and pieces of furniture. Once their belongings were inside, the space shrunk all the more.

Elisabeth remained in the backyard, where she spread a blanket and sat with a book.

"Do you want her to help you?" Sam asked sometime later.

Josie had been bumping into someone everywhere she turned. "No. Let's leave her be for now."

Two ladies who introduced themselves as Ruby Adamson and Vanessa Powell brought savory beef stew and warm corn bread, along with a jug of fresh milk, a pint of cream and butter.

After they ate, Sam put the bed together in the room beside the kitchen. "We'll sleep on pallets until another bed arrives," he told her.

She nodded in agreement. "I'm happy for the girls to have the bed."

Their trunks lined each wall of the parlor. Feeling overwhelmed, Josie was studying the chaos when Sam said, "I'm going to take a few things over to the church."

He hadn't asked her to join him, so she nodded and watched him go.

"May we take baths?" Anna asked.

Josie agreed that bathing sounded like a marvelous idea, and went in search of the water source.

Having bathed with warm water and dressed in their nightclothes for the first time in a week, the girls snuggled together in the only bed that had made the trip with them, the walnut four-poster they'd brought from Philadelphia. The bureau wouldn't fit in the room, so it sat outside their door in the kitchen.

Josie left a lantern burning on the kitchen wall, so if one of them awoke in the strange place, they wouldn't be frightened.

She warmed milk and poured herself a glass. Carrying it out of doors, she sat on the top step.

The evening was already cool. She would need to unpack her shawls. Light illuminated one of the arched windows at the church, and she surmised the room beyond was a study.

She felt as discouraged as she had the night before, so she told herself she'd known what she was doing by accompanying Sam. She was here for the girls. She'd gone along with that.

Standing and walking away from the house, she turned and looked up at the dark, pine-covered mountain. They could do some exploring soon. She liked the crisp, clean scent in the air and the way the heavens seemed so close. The stars twinkled overhead like a thousand diamonds, the moon a pale globe in their midst.

An hour or so later, the sound of the front door opening and closing woke her. She'd been fast asleep on a thick padding of quilts and blankets, and she rose on one elbow. Sam eased open the door with a creak. "Didn't mean to wake you."

"It's all right."

Easing off his boots, he set them against the wall. He blew out the lantern she'd placed on a crate in the corner, and his clothing rustled.

"Is the church nice?" she asked.

"It's more adequate than the house."

Those quiet words assured her he wasn't as unaffected as he'd behaved in front of the girls.

"I'm sorry, Josie," he said. "I'm sure you were expecting more. You're used to much nicer accommodations. As soon as I've had time to settle into my position and make some headway, I'll see what I can do."

"Don't worry about the house, Sam. You've got more important things to focus on right now."

"Thanks for understanding."

She was feeling disconnected…and left out. She should have gone with him to the church, rather than hanging back, but she'd felt awkward about joining him uninvited. "The girls are going to do just fine," she told him. "They've been through a lot. Now they'll have time to get comfortable with the town and turn their thoughts forward. Once we're all settled, we'll get them in school."

"Thank you, Josie."

"Please don't thank me. I want to be here, and I want to be a real part of their lives. Yours, too, if you'll let me."

He recognized how hard Josie was trying. He hadn't realized how much Carrie had handled, or the extent of the sacrifices she'd made until she was gone. He didn't intend to make the same mistake over again.

Sam's emotions conflicted so often that, admittedly, he hadn't been handling things well. Josie was doing her best to fulfill her part of their arrangement. He hadn't made any wild promises to her or expressed his devotion—it was still too soon—but he had entered into a holy commitment. And already he cared deeply for this woman.

In order for this to work, their marriage must be a marriage in more than name only. He had every intention of honoring all the aspects that their commitment entailed.

By the end of the week it was apparent that the house was woefully inadequate. While Sam was busy meeting with the town council, overseeing a newly formed advisory board and studying for his first sermon, Josie instructed the girls to help each other iron their dresses and prepare for an outing.

Eager for any opportunity to escape the confines of the little house, they joined her outside.

"Where are we going?" Anna asked.

"Your father is extremely busy and has important things on his mind," she told them. "There are things we can do to make his duties and all of our lives easier. We'll take care of things on our own and not bother him with domestic details." That was, after all, why he'd needed her. "I need all of you to help me."

"Are we going shopping?" Abigail asked.

"That we are," Josie replied. "We're shopping for a house."

Elisabeth's eyes lit up, delighting Josie no end. "A *bigger* house?"

"Definitely a bigger house. I know the good people of this town intended to do well by us, but a home needs to be a place of comfort and safety, as well as a place to invite friends and the community."

Delighted, the sisters shared hugs and pleased smiles. Anna grasped Josie's hand and led them toward Main Street. "Where do we find a house?"

Sam had spoken to the girls about being content, and he was doing his best to set an example.

She wanted to make things easier for him at home, so they would have more time together as a couple and as a family. If he had time to devote to a search and if he wasn't concerned about money, he would have done this himself. She was grateful that a large-enough house was something she could do for all of them. Josie led them to a building with a real estate sign hanging from its porch. The door was open, so they entered.

A woman sweeping the floor glanced up in surprise. "Well, good morning! What can I do for you?"

"We need to buy a home," Josie told her.

She propped the broom against a wall. "You need to speak with my husband," she answered. "I'll get him straightaway."

An hour later they had seen four homes, and none of them had impressed Josie as being what they needed. The one that came closest was too far from the church.

"There's only one house near the church," Thomas Payne told her as they sat in his canopied buggy. "And it belonged to a man who owned the mill. His wife had family money."

"May we see it?" Josie asked.

"I'm afraid it's not really a preacher's house." His tone was apologetic.

"Why not? It can always be redecorated if it doesn't suit our tastes."

"Oh, no, ma'am, it looks fine. It's just that—well, it has a pretty hefty price tag."

"Oh. How much?"

He told her, but she wasn't deterred. "All right. Show us, please."

Mr. Payne's eyebrows shot up. He lifted the reins to set the horse in motion. He led them past the church and their crowded bungalow, then turned the corner onto a tree-lined street that slowly inclined. At the top of the hill was a house set back from the street, the lot edged by shrubbery and mature trees.

When Josie spotted the colorfully asymmetrical house, anticipation had her leaning forward and taking in every elaborate detail. The gabled house presented an interesting arrangement of bay windows, balconies, stained glass, turrets, porches, brackets and ornamental masonry.

The structure was two-storied, except for a third story at the top of one pointed turret. Someone had painted the ornate trim a garish pink and black, but the wood siding was a cream color, the shingles on the gables a soft bluish green. The steeply pitched, uneven roof was a pale gray.

The fanciful structure stood silhouetted against the lush green pines on the hillside behind. Even though the house sat above most of the town, it was protected by the shadow of the mountain behind.

Josie loved the place the moment she saw it.

Anna squealed and leaped from the buggy to run toward the gate. Abigail and Elisabeth followed, their skirts flying.

Mr. Payne opened the gate, and the sisters dashed up stairs made of huge slabs of stone to wait impatiently on the shaded front porch.

The man held out his brass key ring and fumbled until he found the correct key. Anna's boots clattered in the foyer as she ran forward and came to a stop. With a rising surge of hope, Josie took in the large foyer.

The first floor comprised a drawing room with a stone fireplace, a spacious dining room, a roomy kitchen with a pump and sink and a front parlor that sat in a three-sided bay.

Five bedrooms and a sunroom were on the second floor, and the third-floor room could only be reached by dropping down a trapdoor with a ladder. It was a charming but odd-shaped room, with two windows on each of four sides. Two walls sloped, the others were gabled dormers.

"Can this be my room?" Anna asked with excitement lacing her voice.

"If we were to buy this house, I believe the three of you should sleep on the floor below," Josie replied. "This could be your playing and reading and thinking room."

She looked out the windows that faced the

mountain, charmed to see deer on the shaded slopes. "Look!"

When they were finished ogling the countryside in all directions, Josie turned back to find Mr. Payne with a pleased smile on his face.

"It's a ghastly shade of pink," she said to make certain he knew she didn't intend to pay the full price he'd quoted.

"Remedied easily enough," he replied. "Did you note the beautiful floors?"

She had. The previous owners had worn nary a layer from the perfect walnut planks or their varnished sheen. "There is a lot of overgrown shrubbery that needs to be cut away from the foundation," she told him. "And not a flower in sight."

"Your daughters will certainly enjoy that bathing chamber," he assured her.

She didn't doubt that for a moment. "I imagine the previous owner took his stove with him. We would have to invest in a good one."

"Victor Larken, over at the general store, has a couple of the latest models in his back room. And he can order anything that strikes your fancy."

"I imagine that would cost a pretty penny."

The girls followed them down the ladderlike stairs and into the hall below. "Why don't you admire the scenery while Mr. Payne and I have a talk?" she said to Elisabeth.

Elisabeth nodded and ushered her sisters into one of the bedrooms.

Downstairs again, Josie pointed out wallpaper she didn't care for in the drawing room, and found the door leading to the pantry had no brass knob to match the plate.

After learning she intended to pay with cashier's checks and didn't need a loan, Thomas Payne lowered the price. He cheerfully took them to the bank where she made arrangements and then on to the telegraph office. Later she signed a couple of papers before she and the girls headed for the general store.

"Papa's sure gonna be surprised, isn't he?" Anna asked.

"I expect he will," she answered with a smile.

Elisabeth paused on the boardwalk in front of the store with a question. "Will we each have our own room?"

Josie nodded.

"We don't have curtains for all those windows," she said with a frown.

"We can make curtains," Josie assured her. "But I don't believe that room in the tower needs any, do you?"

"When are we moving in?" Abigail asked.

"I have a little more business to take care of first," Josie told her. "Banking and signing papers."

"Does Papa have to sign the papers?"

"I'll buy it and put his name on it," she explained. "We won't have to trouble him with the details."

"When are we going to tell him?" Elisabeth asked.

"When do you want to tell him?"

Elisabeth appeared thoughtful. "I suppose we could wait until all the business is done."

Abigail and Elisabeth glanced at each other. "Let's surprise him when it's ready," Abigail suggested. "We can move in the furniture and everything first. It will be a grand surprise that way."

"I'll hire the men who are delivering our things from the train station to take them to the new house," Josie agreed with a joyful grin.

Elisabeth turned to look down at Anna. "Can you keep this absolutely secret?"

"Oh, yes! Papa will love our surprise!"

With all of them in agreement, they entered the store. It was the first time Josie had seen all three of them looking so pleased and hopeful. At last she'd been able to do something that made a difference.

Chapter Fourteen

On Sunday, Sam preached his first sermon to the people of Jackson Springs. The pews were filled to capacity, as all the church members and other curious citizens showed up to meet the Harts.

Josie couldn't have been prouder than to be introduced as Sam's wife. Even Elisabeth put on a smile and greeted parishioners cordially.

After the service, the men arranged makeshift tables in the lot behind the church. The ladies served food and drinks, chatting all the while. The men set up a croquet game, and then stood watching the children.

Josie recognized that people and traditions were pretty much the same, wherever a person traveled, with men and women dividing into separate groups, and the children frolicking in the grass.

She studied the hillside, where she still hadn't had time to explore.

"What are you thinking?" Sam had come up beside her.

"Oh!" She gave him a warm smile. "I was thinking about walking through the trees up there. You can see deer from—"

She caught herself before she gave away too much. "From here if you squint."

He squinted. "You have excellent eyes. I don't see any deer."

"Well, maybe it was just the wind moving in the pines."

She glanced at him, and their eyes met.

He gave her a warm smile.

Now that they were here and he had the position he'd been called to, things were less strained between them. She didn't expect flowery expressions of devotion or demonstrative gestures. They were living together as man and wife. They shared a marriage bed. He came home every evening, and they spent family time together. He was kind and considerate. It was more than she'd ever had.

It was more than she'd hoped to have.

Josie wanted to capture every precious moment and enjoy it for all it was worth. At last she had a family to care for and to love. Loneliness was a thing of the past, and she had no regrets about making this choice.

She often wondered how Reverend Martin was doing, and she had written him twice already, to let him know they'd arrived safely. When she thought of her former life and of Margaretta, she felt sadness for the woman who had made her son her whole life. She had excluded others to such an extreme that, once Bram was gone, she had nothing.

"What are you thinking?" Sam asked from beside her.

"I was thinking how blessed I am that God brought you to Reverend Martin's door."

Then he did something altogether unexpected. He reached to take her hand, lacing his fingers through hers and said, "We are the ones who were blessed."

She remembered how the mothers and daughters had flocked around him in Durham. "You could have had your choice of young women, once you got here."

"But once again, God saw the bigger picture and pointed out the wisdom of asking you."

She had asked God to take away her desire for a family, but the acute desire had never diminished. Now she knew why. Sam didn't know he was the answer to her prayers.

Josie enjoyed the knowledge that she was able to give something to Sam in return. She imagined his reaction to the house, and prayed he would love it as much as she and the girls did. He'd done a good job of covering up his disappointment over the parsonage.

Enjoying the strength and warmth of his hand holding hers, she looked up into his blue eyes.

"Do you miss Nebraska?" he asked.

"I think about the reverend from time to time, but no. There's no comparison to being here and having a full life with a family."

His gaze dropped to her lips, and her heart lifted with the anticipation of a kiss. She glanced to the side, noting that they stood in full view of their new neighbors and parishioners.

"Hold that thought," he said, surprising her, and the corner of his mouth tilted upward.

"How do you know what I'm thinking?"

"You're blushing."

"Perhaps it's the sun."

"Perhaps."

Their eyes met and locked. His were surprisingly warm.

"I expect some other man would have claimed you for his wife if I hadn't asked first."

Not wanting to draw unwanted attention, she turned and faced the children playing croquet. "Actually, you didn't ask first."

Sam's fingers tightened around hers. "What? What do you mean?"

"Someone else asked me before you did."

Sam didn't let her view the crowd, but tugged her hand until she faced him. "Who? Did I meet him?"

"You met him. It was Reverend Martin."

"Henry?" he asked, his eyebrows climbing his forehead. "But you refused him?"

"Not at first. I was thinking strongly about accepting."

"Why didn't you?"

"Because before I could, you asked me."

His expression revealed he was plainly disconcerted. He looked aside, but she could tell he wasn't actually seeing anything. He was thinking over what she'd just revealed.

"I told him the truth."

His wordless gaze shot to hers.

"That I couldn't marry him because you had asked me, and I'd accepted."

"You chose us over him? Over staying in your hometown and with your friends."

"As you'll recall, it didn't take me long to make a decision."

Indeed, Sam recalled her acceptance. At the time, he'd been so focused on the mission that he hadn't stopped to analyze or imagine her reasoning. She'd agreed to come, and he'd been relieved.

Now he was grateful, and perhaps a little ashamed for plowing ahead with his plans and not stopping to look at her needs or her desires.

He'd done the same thing with Carrie, uprooting her and moving her from her safe, comfortable home, into the dangerous land that had taken her life. Sam determined in his heart that he would not take Josie for granted, nor would he make her regret her decision to marry him and start over in a new land.

He would do everything in his power to take care of her the way she was taking care of his daughters.

* * *

The following week passed rapidly. Sam did most of his calling during the day hours, but he was trying to meet everyone in the first couple of weeks, so he traveled each evening.

Josie recognized that his daughters missed him when he went calling, and understood what that was like. She took special care to fill those hours with activities and studies. She reminded them often that their father loved them and would be home for their bedtime.

They used two of those evenings to scamper to the new house, where they swept and washed and dusted in preparation for the arrival of their trunks and furniture.

During the day, they sewed new curtains and worked on the quilt Josie had begun. Elisabeth preferred the curtains to the quilt work, and her stitches were straight and even, so Josie merely supervised.

She hired a painter and selected a color for the outside trim, but the man and his son would be unable to come until the following week.

On the day their belongings were due to arrive, Josie spotted two wagons in front of the tiny parsonage.

She ran out and glanced toward the church, hoping Sam wasn't near a window. "Those aren't to be delivered here," she told the dusty man driving the first wagon.

"Man at the station told me to find you here," he replied.

"Yes, he was right about that. But everything goes to a different house. If you turn the wagons around and head up that last street you passed, the house is at the top of the hill. You can't miss it. It's trimmed in pink. I'll be right behind you."

"Pink?" he asked.

"Let me get my girls and I'll meet you there."

Laughing and giggling, the Hart sisters accompanied her up the hill.

"I hope your father didn't see us leave," Josie said.

"He's gone this morning," Elisabeth assured her. "He asked if I wanted to come along, but I knew today was the day, so I said no."

The two fellows were tired and thirsty, so Josie sent Elisabeth back to the house for supplies to make lemonade in the new kitchen.

It became clear to Josie that the two men weren't able to work fast enough to have all the furniture unloaded and settled in the appropriate rooms by supper, so she hurried into town and located a couple of young men to accompany her back and join the hauling process.

It was a warm afternoon, and there wasn't a person there who didn't show the exertion of their tasks. Josie didn't have time to stop for a breath.

So that she could get back and fix supper, she instructed the men to leave the last several items in the middle of the drawing room and asked the young fellows to come back the next day.

She paid each one what he was due and they hurried home.

Supper was a feast of quickly sliced ham and fried eggs.

"Ab, your hair looks as though you tangled with a mountain lion today," Sam said jokingly.

"Oh, yes." Abigail reached up in a useless attempt to smooth her braid. "I must have forgotten to brush it."

"You all look a little red-faced this evening."

Josie tried to remember if she'd checked her appearance in the mirror after she'd changed into fresh clothing. None of the females met each other's eyes or Sam's. No one said a word. If pressed, the girls would not lie.

"The sun must have been hot today," he commented. "Were you outdoors?"

"We did go out," Josie replied for all of them. "And the sun was quite warm."

"I've been gone several evenings," he began.

"If you have someone to call on, Father, you go right ahead," Elisabeth told him. "We don't mind a bit. We understand you're introducing yourself to all the new people."

He was still for a moment. "I'd invite them here if I could."

"It's okay, Papa," Abigail seconded. "Josie keeps us busy while you're away."

"We got a whole *lotta* work to do," Anna said with a nod.

Josie stood quickly. "Mrs. Powell brought us a jar of her applesauce. Why don't we have some for dessert?"

She unwrapped oatmeal cookies they'd baked the day before and served them with the applesauce.

Sam excused himself to the outbuilding to wash and shave before he went calling.

"You almost *told*," Abigail chastised her little sister.

"No, I did not," Anna argued.

"Come, let's do the dishes so we can hurry up the hill as soon as he leaves." Josie stacked their plates.

The mood was quite conspiratorial as they whisked the dishes from the sudsy water through the rinse pan, Elisabeth drying and putting them away.

When Sam returned, dressed in a fresh white shirt and a black tie, wearing black trousers, the handsome sight took Josie's breath away.

His daughters, preoccupied and used to seeing him dressed so, gave him dismissive hugs and kisses.

After they'd scampered back to their tasks, he paused and studied Josie with uncertainty. He was clearly uncomfortable and questioning how to handle the moment.

Sparing him a decision, she stepped toward him just as each of his daughters had done and pressed her cheek to his. He smelled of shaving soap and starch, and the scent gave her strangely contradictory feelings of longing and satisfaction. His cheek was smooth and warm, and he turned his face to press a kiss against her temple.

"Have a nice evening," he said against her ear.

A tingle of appreciation passed along her nerve endings. "And you, as well."

He stepped back, his gaze roaming her hair, coming back to her eyes, but settling on her lips. He kissed her then, in the middle of the kitchen, with the girls only a few feet behind him. They fell uncharacteristically silent. He released her slowly, holding her hands in his large warm ones, and looking at her as though he'd just noticed something.

"Is something wrong?" she asked.

He smiled and ran his thumb along her jaw, framed her face and kissed her again, this time with so much feeling that her head felt faint when he released her. "Everything's right," he whispered.

Joyful tears stung behind her eyelids, but she smiled.

Sam turned and left the kitchen.

Josie stood with her heart pounding. Sam's kisses set her heart aflutter and left her wondering what he was thinking.

Anna came to stand beside Josie, curling her fingers into hers. Abigail trailed after her father and returned a minute later. "He's gone."

Elisabeth continued to observe Josie with a reserved expression. Josie met her eyes and gave her a hesitant smile. It must be difficult for her to see Josie in the position that had once been her mother's.

Elisabeth looked away.

Josie removed her apron. "Let's go!"

They shot into action, gathering the items they'd stashed to take with them, and left the little house to climb the hill.

"I still can't believe this is our house," Abigail said with a giggle, dancing ahead through the gate and up the stone steps.

"Do we have room for a lamb now?" Anna asked with all seriousness.

"You are going to have to take that up with your papa," Josie answered.

The foyer was cluttered with crates and cartons and odds and ends that had been dropped in their hurry, but it looked wonderful to her. She loved the high-ceilinged entry, the magnificent sweeping staircase with its curving banister and the ornate lamp that hung a good six feet above them.

"How do you light that?" Abigail asked.

"I have no idea," Josie answered. She turned and surveyed the mess, then the girls. "All right." She gathered her thoughts. "Let's work on putting away as much as we can in the kitchen and the dining room. Tomorrow, when our helpers come to get the rest of our things up the stairs for us, we'll do the bedrooms."

The men had situated her china hutch and sideboard in the dining room. Kneeling, Josie opened crates to inspect her dishes.

"We brought china, too." Elisabeth stood to the

side, her fingers laced in front of her. "There's a set that were Mother and Father's wedding gift."

Josie paused to look from Elisabeth to the other girls, taking note of their concern. The things they'd brought with them from Pennsylvania were all they had left of their mother and their former life. "Why don't we put those in this cabinet so you can see them?" Josie said. "Mine aren't particularly special. I can keep them in the kitchen, for everyday dishes."

Though Elisabeth had been careful with her expression, Josie took note of the way she relaxed her posture and nodded. Had she thought Josie wouldn't want her mother's things in sight?

"What about Mama's tea set?" Anna came and leaned against Josie, where she knelt beside the crate.

Quite naturally, Josie put her arm around the child and pulled her close in an easy embrace, while she glanced about. "I have the perfect place. How about right smack dab in the center of the sideboard there? The sun will hit the china as it comes through the windows."

She settled the lid back on the crate and stood to look around. "Which trunk do you supposed holds your mama's china and tea set?"

"These two are ours," Abigail told her, pointing.

They opened the trunk and found dishes carefully packed between clothing items and baby clothes.

"Those were ours," Anna told her. "There's a

dress and bonnet that each of us wore. Mama said she would keep them forever."

Josie held up the miniature white dresses, meticulously stitched and embroidered. She imagined Sam's wife tenderly touching them as she packed, reminiscing about the sweet babies she'd borne and nursed and rocked. "I'll bet you were the most beautiful babies in Philadelphia." She laid them out, pressing the wrinkles with a reverent touch. "I'll iron them and we can put them safely away in the trunk. Do you know whose is whose?"

Abigail frowned. "They all look alike."

"Maybe Father will know," Elisabeth suggested.

"Yes, maybe," Josie agreed.

She placed the dinnerware in the cabinet, relieved that all the pieces had made the journey safely. "Your mama did a good job packing these."

When all the pieces had been unpacked and put away, they stood back to admire their handiwork. The girls grew silent.

"Remember, it's good to talk about your mother if you want to," Josie told them.

"I remember washing these dishes with Mama," Abigail said.

"They will be our Sunday dishes," Josie assured her.

After pushing the trunks against the wall, they took a last look and moved into the kitchen.

Josie didn't want any of them to think she was trying to replace their mother or that she felt her place was any more important than Carrie's had been. Carrie was their mother, and it would always be that way. She hoped her actions showed that she valued their feelings.

Exhausted, they spent the following evening at home, not finishing until the day after and finalizing their plans to surprise Sam.

"It has to be during the day that we bring him," Elisabeth said. "So he can see the mountain from the turret."

Josie agreed wholeheartedly.

On Thursday morning, Josie and the girls exchanged conspiratorial looks at breakfast. Josie poured Sam a cup of coffee and nodded at Elisabeth.

"We have a surprise for you," she told her father.

"I love surprises." He sipped his coffee and studied Elisabeth over the rim of the cup. "What is it?"

Chapter Fifteen

"We have to show you," Abigail said, grinning from ear to ear.

"Well, I'm ready." He set down his cup. "Shall I close my eyes? Have you sewn another quilt square?"

Anna giggled. "No-o," she said, drawing the word out in mischief. "It's a lot bigger than that."

"If you're finished eating, we'll show you," Josie said.

Sam followed, hesitating every so often, as though he expected them to pull something out from behind them.

"It's not *here*," Abigail said. "We have to take you to it."

Out of doors, the pine-scented mountain breeze lifted all their hair as it rustled the sleeves of Sam's white shirt.

Abigail and Anna each took one of his hands and practically pulled him up the hill.

"Are we going to climb that whole mountain?" he asked in mock concern.

"Just a little farther," Anna told him.

Josie enjoyed the look of anticipation on Elisabeth's face.

Sam recognized the animation and pleasure with which his daughters were orchestrating this outing. He couldn't imagine what they were planning, but they'd been quite preoccupied most of the week. It pleased him to see their lighthearted behavior. He'd been so busy that he had only Josie to thank for the mood she'd created.

He glanced over his shoulder to see she wore a similar expression of expectation. So often when he looked at her, his reaction surprised him. This time he hadn't expected to appreciate the color on her cheeks or notice the sun on her lustrous, dark, wavy hair. When she gazed up at him, something hard and hurting inside him softened a little more.

Her optimism and her outlook made him believe they were going to do all right here in Colorado. She had infinite patience with Anna's never-ending questions and encouragement for Abigail's moments of sadness and loss. She handled Elisabeth's resentment with kindness and understanding.

She met his eyes and something warm and undeniably affectionate passed between them. Something he wasn't expecting, and it made him look forward to time alone with her.

"A little farther!" Anna called out.

Sam turned his attention to the street. "What have you females cooked up?"

The homes they passed were as nice as any he'd seen in the affluent neighborhoods back east, most with flower gardens and some with carriage houses.

As they reached the crest of the hill, they came to a halt before a large house with garish pink trim. He stared at the house, then turned to his daughters and Josie. They glanced from the sight before them to his face with expectancy.

Sam couldn't have been more confused. "Do we know someone who lives here?"

Anna and Abigail giggled. "Yes!" they chorused.

Elisabeth opened the gate, and they towed him up the thick stone stairs bordered by foliage. "Who?" he asked.

They urged him toward the porch and Anna released his hand to dance around him.

Still puzzled, he climbed the stairs. "Who lives here?"

Adding to his surprise, Josie produced a key and proceeded to insert it into the lock and turn it. The door opened, and the younger girls rushed forward into the interior.

Confused, Sam looked at Elisabeth, who simply gestured for him to enter.

"Who lives here?" he asked again.

"We do!" they shouted together, and their voices echoed in the foyer.

Sam glanced around the entryway, feeling decidedly off-kilter. Nothing looked familiar, but neither was there any home owner rushing to discover who had entered his house. "Would someone mind explaining?"

"It's *our* house, Papa!" Anna told him.

"We bought it and brought all our stuff here," Abigail explained. "Wait 'til you see!"

Sam looked to Josie for confirmation, and she nodded with a smile. "It's ours."

"Come look!" Anna took his hand and pulled him along the hallway, past a room full of unfamiliar furniture to a dining room with more unfamiliar furniture. The girls had rushed in ahead, but now they parted, giving him a view of a cabinet filled with dishes.

He recognized the plates and bowls as being the same set they'd had at home. His gaze traveled until it lit upon the dainty, violet-sprigged tea set arranged before the window, and the facts fell together. Carrie's teapot and cups.

He looked beyond the room to the one beside it, and a rocking chair immediately caught his attention. He walked toward it, into a small room with a few trunks still stacked against a wall.

He reached out and gently set the familiar rocker into motion. Carrie had rocked every one of their daughters in this chair and had insisted it come west with them for future generations of Harts. These were their things.

"Show him the rest of the house," Josie suggested.

They gave him a tour of the spacious kitchen, with a brand-new cast-iron stove, the bathing chamber and the drawing room.

Upstairs, the rooms were not completely furnished. When they showed him the largest bedroom, he recognized that the bureau and wardrobe held his own clothing, which had been in one of the trunks they'd brought with them.

The shock had him thinking too slowly. "Where did all of this other furniture come from?"

Josie clasped her hands together. "I had most of it shipped, you'll remember. We picked out a few ready-made pieces at a furniture maker's in town. Of course, if there's anything you don't like, we can exchange it."

"I knew you shipped your belongings, but I had no idea there was…so much."

They now stood in the wide upstairs hallway.

"I hope you don't mind that I kept nearly everything." She gestured to a narrow table against a wall. "That was from my father's study."

"Everything is quite…*nice*."

"Not *too* much?" she asked, a wrinkle of concern creasing her forehead. "Don't you like it?"

"It's not that I don't like it," he said, bringing one hand up to his jaw in thought.

"Look at the room above," Elisabeth suggested.

They took him up ladderlike stairs to a room with a breathtaking view of the mountainside. Anna pointed out deer trails. He couldn't imagine how they'd gotten the few chairs up here. The girls' books were stored neatly in two small crates turned on their sides and an oil lamp sat atop the stack.

She'd bought a house. A very nice, very *expensive* house.

When the girls disappeared down the stairs, he turned to her and asked in a low voice, "Did the bank give us a loan?"

She shook her head. "The house is paid for. It's in your name." She raised a hand to her throat in a nervous gesture. "I have the deed for you."

"You paid for it?"

"Yes. I assure you there's no debt."

"And the stove and the new furnishings?"

"Paid for, as well. Cash."

Surprised, he called down, "Give us a moment, please."

Josie's caramel-brown eyes widened as she studied him.

"How did you afford it?"

"I had accounts transferred to the local bank. The local banker was quite accommodating."

Of course he was. "I know how funds are transferred," he said, keeping his voice calm. "What I don't know is how you happened to have so much of it to throw around."

"I told you I sold my house in Durham."

Granted, he'd only seen the outside of that house, and it was fine indeed, but this one surpassed that. "You told me you spent that money on shipping our things."

"Not all of it. And I had more, besides. I sold the newspaper. I got a modest down payment, and I'll be getting a payment each month. It will be plenty to live on, if you're concerned about the upkeep of the house. And remember that the board will pay us a housing allowance."

He shook his head, absorbing the information.

"I have other accounts that are still untouched," she added matter-of-factly.

Other accounts? He leveled a gaze on her.

"My father left me an inheritance," she explained with a shrug. "As did my first husband."

Sam felt as though he'd been sucker punched. He opened his mouth, but couldn't breathe for several seconds. Finally he drew in a breath and released it. "You're—rich."

She blinked at him. "I've always been blessed with more than I need, it's true. But I'm not foolish, nor do I value earthly things above treasures in heaven. Whatever I have became yours when we married. We have enough to live comfortably."

"And you never bothered to mention this?"

"It never came up. It wasn't important."

"Well, it's pretty important to me."

She clasped her hands. "I'm sorry. I didn't deliberately keep the money a secret."

"It seems as though you did all this without telling me because you knew I wouldn't approve."

Her expression showed surprise at his words. "That's not why we didn't tell you. You have important matters to handle. We didn't want to distract you with trivial details." Her eyes filled with tears. "Sam, you don't approve?"

He rubbed his forehead and tried to think without letting her tears affect him. She always spoke so rationally, and she never failed to consider decisions with a spiritual perspective. The irony of that wasn't lost on him—him, the man of God. "You heard what I told my daughters when they complained about that little house."

"Yes," she whispered. "I thought you were making the best of the situation. I didn't think you wouldn't want another house, if it were possible. I never dreamed you would disapprove." She shrugged in a self-deprecating manner. "I guess that was foolish."

"It's not that I don't approve of you or even the house," he began. How could he have missed the fact that she had a lot more money? He'd known about her house and remembered something about her husband working at the newspaper. Inheritances were news. But then he'd never thought to ask.

"Papa?" Anna called from downstairs. "Are you ready to see the outside in the back?"

"I should be the one providing for you and for my daughters," he told her, feeling as though he'd failed them. He could never have done all this on his salary.

"I didn't stop to think of it like that," she said. "God is our Provider, Sam. We wouldn't have any of this if He hadn't seen fit to give it to me. I consider it a blessing, and I never thought you'd see it any other way."

Well, yes, there it was, her straightforward reliance on God, with nary a glance to the left or the right. There was no way he could argue with her reasoning, and he'd be a fool to try. Of course she looked to God as her Provider, and of course His wisdom was greater than theirs. "I should have been in on a decision of such magnitude."

"Yes, of course."

The question crept into his head about the reaction of the townspeople. Would they question such extravagance or wonder at its source? It would be his own fault for overlooking these details and being in such a hurry to marry Josie and get her here that he hadn't cared to learn more.

"Go ahead." He gestured to the stairs. She gathered her skirts and descended ahead of him.

All the joy she'd taken in seeing the girls' pleasure and planning the surprise was gone, leaving Josie feeling she'd disappointed her husband.

Elisabeth appeared concerned over her father's lack of enthusiasm, but the other girls hadn't seemed to notice.

Abigail led the way through the kitchen and out of doors. Sam lifted his gaze to the verdant hillside and stood studying the landscape.

"Can we bring our bed and sleep here tonight?" Anna asked.

Josie said nothing.

Elisabeth looked at her, then at her father.

"I want to know why this house is significant," Sam said at last. He turned to Anna first. "Why is this particular house so important to you?"

Anna scrunched her nose for a minute as she thought, then said, "'Cause we got all our own stuff and our own rooms and a big, big yard. See how big this yard is, Papa?"

"I see that," he answered. "Ab?"

Abigail seemed a trifle caught off guard by the question. "This house is important because…we can have all of Mama's things here, and we can all sit at the table in the dining room on Sundays."

Sam nodded and turned to his oldest daughter.

"We thought you would be pleased," she said, obviously taking a more defensive tone. "We don't have enough room in that little house, and this one is nice. It's big enough for all of us. You were busy, so we did all this ourselves."

That last bit could have been interpreted as accusatory, but Sam didn't comment. He turned his gaze on Josie. "What does this house mean to you?"

Chapter Sixteen

It wasn't just the house. This move and this family meant everything to her. "I know the church board meant well by providing the other house. No doubt it was the best they could do, and we're grateful. But here you can hold Bible studies and invite neighbors to dinner. It's a stunning example of just how much God loves us that we can live here and welcome our new friends. I hoped it wouldn't be just a house or a thing. I hoped it would be our *home*." She looked into his eyes and spoke earnestly. "But I would live in a cave if you thought it was best for all of us."

His expression softened, and he shook his head. "A cave won't be necessary." He turned and peered up at the back of the house. "I do recognize how much this means to each of you. I simply don't want any of us to be ungrateful or unappreciative. We have to learn to be content wherever God leads us."

"I don't think God led us to that little house," Abigail said in all seriousness. "I think He had this one waiting. We just didn't know it, and the church people didn't know it."

"Hmm. Do you think God is fond of pink?" Sam asked, still studying the architecture and details.

The girls were quiet for a few seconds, and then Abigail giggled. "God made pink flowers."

"And I saw a bunny with pink eyes once," Anna added.

Josie relaxed marginally. His daughters' comfort and peace of mind meant everything to Sam. She prayed he recognized that she hadn't been thinking selfishly when she'd come up with this idea.

"Painters are coming next week to change the color," she assured him.

He took a step back and shaded his eyes with a hand for a better look. "I could do that myself and save the cost."

Josie's heart leaped into her throat at the thought of Sam on top of the house. She'd spent months taking care of Reverend Martin after a fall from a roof not as high as this one. "Some things are better left to professionals," she said quietly.

He turned and raised an eyebrow.

"Reverend Martin was nearly killed falling from the church roof."

"We'll talk about it."

"Yes, of course."

"We'll talk about a lot of things, so that I don't

have any more surprises." His voice was kind as he asked, "What do you have planned for today?"

"I hoped to move the bed and the rest of our things from the other house."

"I'll help."

The girls crowded around him, exclaiming.

"I need to do *something* to help." His gaze touched each of them, but returned to Josie. "You've been working so hard."

"I just know how busy you are," she said.

When the girls hurried back into the house, they followed more slowly. Sam stopped her with a hand on her arm. "Things that concern the family aren't less worthy of my time than church matters," he told her.

"I know that," she said. "I hope you don't think I was attempting to go around your authority. I simply hoped to make things easier for you."

He tilted his head. "I vow to be more approachable."

But he hadn't actually said he approved of the house or that he was pleased with it. Josie had the feeling that his reluctant acceptance of their move had come about because the girls would have been devastated otherwise. They'd been through too much for him to deliberately disappoint them again.

Josie wished she had the confidence to throw herself into his embrace and find the assurance she craved in his arms. She yearned to do just that. "Our helpers are bringing their wagon," she told him. "I already had it arranged."

"No one will ever call you a helpless female," he said with a grin. "Come on."

Sam took the bed apart and carried the pieces outdoors, in time to greet the two young men who had pulled a wagon up in front of the parsonage.

"Gilbert Stelling, sir." The tallest one extended a hand.

"Will York," said the other.

As Gilbert explained, the two were cousins who worked on a ranch, but they were in town for a holiday. They'd been in the general store the day Josie had been looking for help, and earning a few extra dollars appealed to them.

Will looked to be about fourteen, and Sam noticed that every time Elisabeth carried something out of the house, he took it from her arms.

There really hadn't been that much in the house, and every time Sam ran into a doorjamb or couldn't get out of a room because someone was already standing in the cramped space, he recognized just how tiny the parsonage was and how foolish his recommendation that they make the most of it. He understood why the girls had been so upset. He hadn't wanted to admit the house was too small, because there'd been nothing he could do about it.

Later that afternoon, he watched Josie pay the two young fellows. They climbed onto their wagon seat and rode down the hill.

The Harts ate a cold supper in the new kitchen.

Afterward, Josie made coffee and they lingered around the table.

"We can take baths inside this winter," Elisabeth pointed out.

"That is a very good reason to like this house," he admitted.

"Can we get a lamb now?" Anna asked. She'd likely been waiting several days to ask that question, and her restraint in waiting until now impressed him.

"Lambs grow into sheep very quickly," he told her. "We don't have a barn—or a pasture. A sheep wouldn't be very happy here. Remember Elisabeth telling you about the lady back in Durham who kept a sheep tied up by her door? The poor animal can't be happy living like that."

"I remember," Anna replied in a dejected tone.

"Tomorrow morning we will all go to the schoolhouse to meet your teacher," he said.

Josie got out papers and charcoal sticks and suggested Anna draw pictures. The subject was once again sidetracked.

Sometime later, as they sat in the drawing room together, Anna complained of a stomachache. A look of worry crossed Sam's face, and he turned to Josie. "Do you know what to do for her?"

Josie set down her sewing and stood. "My mama used to have something to fix that right up. Get her ready for bed and I'll be up."

She went into the kitchen and boiled a few peppermint leaves, then added a sprinkling of ginger root. While the liquid was cooling, she found a sock, filled it with dry rice and heated it in the oven.

Anna sipped the warm, fragrant brew from one of Josie's plain stoneware mugs. "Now we'll lie this on your tummy and it will help you feel all better."

Sam turned to where Elisabeth and Abigail perched at the foot of the bed. "Will one of you sleep with Anna tonight?"

"I will," Abigail offered quickly. "I didn't want to sleep alone this first night, anyway."

"I'll stay with them, too," Elisabeth offered.

So that night, the three of them ended up sharing a bed after all.

"Anna might be nervous about attending an unfamiliar classroom," Josie mentioned when she and Sam were alone. "And I wonder how much of her ailment was the thought of sleeping by herself for the first time."

He looked at her dubiously. "Do you really think so?"

"New surroundings can be frightening."

It was such a relief to have someone with whom to share these responsibilities, and especially nice that she was capable and exceedingly kind. "Thank you for knowing what to do. They've never been sick. Not a day I can think of."

Now that she thought about it, her stomach was a little on the queasy side, as well, and she wasn't worried about sleeping alone. Josie made herself the same concoction, sipped it and prayed the family would be spared from sickness.

Late that night, Josie crept silently into the room where Anna lay sleeping with her sisters. They were so beautiful, each of them in their own unique way. She touched Anna's forehead, finding her skin cool. Reassured, she nonetheless knelt at the foot of their bed and prayed.

Sam awakened to find Josie's place beside him empty. Concerned, he rose and pulled on his trousers. Perhaps she'd gone to the kitchen, or maybe he'd missed hearing one of the girls cry out.

His first thought was to look in Abigail's new room, and then he remembered she hadn't slept there. He crossed to Anna's.

In the moonlight, he made out his daughters' silvery pale hair upon their pillows as they lay still and peaceful. Near the foot of the bed knelt another figure, this one with dark hair streaming across a pale white nightgown.

At the sight, emotion swelled within him. He'd done the same thing many times, praying over the children he loved so dearly. Since Carrie's death, he'd never hoped to know another person who loved them so deeply, who was so concerned with their well-being that she would share his devotion.

Yet here she was, this woman God had sent to him. He didn't feel as lost or as lonely as he once had. Humbled, he thanked God for the reminder and the correction. Whenever he overlooked the obvious, whenever he let pride get in the way of what was best, God graciously pointed his foolishness out to him.

A dark and private place inside his heart had begun to open itself to the light. The opening hurt as much as it gave him pleasure, because while this was a beginning, it was also an end. An end to life the way he'd known it—but the start of something rich and beautiful.

"Thank You for waking me up and showing me this," he whispered.

If he looked back over the past weeks, over his days and nights with Josie, he could mark each of the moments that had awakened him to this beginning. Her riding beside him on the wagon seat, the sunlight glistening from her eyelashes. Holding her outside the circle of their campfire, feeling her heart beating against his chest, breathing in the delicate scent of her hair. Josie turning from the sink to greet him, suds dripping from her fingers and a smile curving her rosy lips.

Sam still had a lot of sorting out to do, but he wasn't foolish enough to deny what he was beginning to feel for his wife. He didn't want to miss out on any of the blessings God had in store for him.

Anna was fine the next morning, though Josie continued to sip peppermint tea, and ate only a few bites of the oatmeal she'd prepared.

Miss DeSmet greeted them when they entered

the white schoolhouse. "You must be the Harts!" she said with a broad smile. "I've been expecting you."

The thin woman wore a plain gray skirt and a calico shirtwaist. She had bright red hair pinned in a knot at her nape, and her eyes were a vivid green.

Sam introduced each of them. "The girls will be starting next Monday. We're nearly settled into our home."

"I understand you're living in the big house up behind Church Street."

"Indeed we are," Sam replied.

"The Collins family lives at the foot of the hill. I'll speak with the children today. You can all walk to school together."

"That will be nice, once they get into a routine," Sam told her.

Miss DeSmet showed them which desks they would be using, and explained the curriculum for their age groups.

By the time they left, Josie thought the girls had a good picture of their new school.

A few evenings later, Anna brought up her favorite topic again. They sat in the drawing room where Elisabeth was reading, and Abigail was working on a quilt square.

Anna looked up from her wooden horse figures to ask, "Is a bunny small enough to be happy at our house?"

"Rabbits are wild creatures, Anna," Sam told her.

"What about a brother? Can we have a brother?"

Josie's hands fell still on the hem she was stitching into a curtain.

"We got those little clothes Mama saved."

Sam met Josie's eyes briefly, and his look was apologetic. "Three daughters are a handful. We don't need any more children."

"Some families got lots of brothers and sisters," she persisted.

"Some families do indeed," he agreed. "But this family is big enough just the way it is. Babies take a lot of work, and Josie has her hands full taking care of you."

Josie was relieved at his reply as well as his certainty that he didn't want more children. She would have struggled, had she known she was disappointing him.

"We received an invitation for tea at a neighbor's next Saturday," she told the girls. "All of our names were included, so we have an outing to plan."

Abigail set her sewing aside. "What will I wear?"

"One of your church dresses will suit the occasion," Josie told her, already knowing Abigail would dearly love to wear dresses that hadn't belonged to her older sister. "We'll come up with something."

The following morning, Josie suggested they go into town and shop for fabric and patterns. They may not have new dresses in time for the tea if they had to order from a catalog, but they could work on them for future events. "We need to think about clothing for school, as well," she reminded them.

"We didn't make our own clothes at home," Elisabeth told her.

"Well, you can learn now," she replied.

"I want to sew," Abigail said brightly.

The general store carried only a small selection of serviceable fabrics, and very few patterns. Victor Larken suggested they visit the dressmaker across the street, who had a room of fabric, scrap and trim in her shop.

Opal Zimmerman was a tiny little lady with a surprisingly booming voice that caught Josie off guard. She hadn't met her in church, but there was another denomination where a portion of the townspeople worshipped, so it was possible she attended there.

"We're going to make dresses ourselves, and Mr. Larken suggested you might have suitable fabric we'd be interested in."

Opal ushered them into her side room. "He doesn't have much of a selection, does he? Once I discovered that, I started ordering and keeping pretty fabric in stock. Some seasons, I can't keep up." She opened the front shutters. "I keep these closed so the material doesn't fade. There's a selection of patterns in those drawers back there. They've all been used. If you have any to trade, I'll trade or give you credit."

Josie found several patterns she thought she could alter to make them more fashionable, and she let the girls select their own colors and trim.

"We will work on one dress at a time," Josie told them as they left the shop.

"Abigail may have her dress first," Elisabeth offered.

Abigail squealed and danced around them. "Maybe it will be ready in time for the tea!"

They stopped so Josie could make a purchase at the butcher's, and then they hurried home.

Sam arrived to the delectable scent of savory beef cooking. The women had turned the dining room into a dressmaking shop. Spools of thread, scissors and bolts of colorful fabric covered the length of the table. His first thought was that they could never have managed this at the little house, but his next reaction was to consider the source of all the material on display.

"We went shopping today!" Abigail told him. "Look! I'm getting a new dress for the tea! It's blue like my eyes, and it has these tiny little pink roses in the stripes. Isn't it going to be beautiful?"

"Indeed," he replied. "Didn't we talk about your dresses lasting another season?"

"But Josie's teaching us how to sew our own," Abigail explained. "She said it's not nearly as expensive as having a dressmaker do it."

"Do you *need* these dresses, or are they something you wanted because they're pretty and new?"

"Oh, we needed them, Papa," Abigail assured him. "We go to school on Monday, and we have a tea to attend. I won't have to wear all of Elisabeth's old dresses now. And Elisabeth's dresses are getting too short on her."

Sam glanced at Elisabeth where she stood beside the table. Her ankles were indeed showing under the hem of her dress.

"Did you open an account?" he asked Josie.

She took straight pins from her mouth to reply. "Oh no, I paid for the supplies we got today."

She was wearing a soft, rose-colored shirtwaist with ruffles down the front, and a deep brown skirt. She always dressed impeccably and often wore clothing he'd never seen. Plenty of her trunks must have contained clothing.

She'd been a pretty young widow, with enough money to keep her living comfortably for the rest of her life when she'd accepted his proposal. Sometimes he wondered why she'd said yes to him rather than Reverend Martin. She was used to more than he had to offer, but that didn't really matter, since she could take care of herself.

And his daughters.

Seeing their pleasure with the house and their rooms and this clothing assured him they had what they needed. He'd done the best for them that he'd known how, though his desire for them had been Josie's nurturing, not her money.

And she was nurturing. Kindhearted, loving—all the things a mother should be. If her only flaw was spoiling them, he could overlook that.

He wondered why the thought of her being able to provide all this bothered him, and again he scoffed at how he hadn't noticed the fact that she had so much money before she bought the house.

Maybe he hadn't wanted to know. Sam had never inquired about financial details. *He hadn't been paying attention.* If he'd paid as much attention to her as she did to him and the girls, he would have known.

As he considered his neglect, he supposed he wouldn't have proposed to her if he'd known how truly well off she was—or that Henry had asked her first. He would've felt foolish for offering her a life with far less than she was accustomed to.

Maybe she hadn't settled.

Maybe it was best he hadn't known of her wealth.

The image of her kneeling at the foot of Anna's bed came to him then, forcing him to compare his feelings of inadequacy to her unselfish devotion.

He'd known she was perfect for his daughters because of her kindness and her faith. The fact that his new wife had come with a lot of money was taking some adjustment. He'd been confident about her suitability, partly because of her generosity, so it only stood to reason that she'd be openhanded with her money.

As surely as he knew his own name, he knew the obstacle standing in his way was pride.

The fact that she could provide the means to make their lives better and easier wouldn't bother him, if it weren't for his stubborn male pride. "'A man's pride shall bring him low, but honor shall uphold the humble in spirit,'" he quoted aloud to remind himself.

He loved the book of Proverbs for its straightforward wisdom. Sometimes he could even laugh at the irony of the analogies Solomon had made. This had been the first verse that popped into his head, but he wasn't laughing now.

"What does that mean, Papa?" Anna asked.

"It means a man's pride will drag him down."

"But you're proud of us, aren't you?"

"That's a good kind of pride. I'm proud to be a child of the living God. I'm proud to be your father. The pride that we shouldn't allow in our hearts is the kind that puffs us up, or that stands in the way of our being humble."

"I don't understand," she said with a frown.

"That's okay. You don't need to think on it."

But *he* did. He needed to think on it a lot.

Chapter Seventeen

Constance Graham entertained half a dozen women and as many of their daughters on her shaded front porch. She was a rancher's daughter who had married a banker and moved to Jackson Springs several years ago.

"I have two sons," she told Josie. "They're rowdy and loud, and I couldn't invite you here if they weren't off working. I have to keep my tea things under lock and key so they aren't trampled in the daily stampede."

Previously, Josie had met Ruby Adamson and Vanessa Powell, but now she was introduced to Melissa Larken.

"Like Mr. Larken at the general store?" Josie asked.

Melissa's eyes were bright and her complexion glowing. She was expecting a baby very soon. "He's my father-in-law. My husband is the deputy sheriff."

Arlene Stelling introduced herself. "Over there are my daughters, Libby and Patience."

The two young ladies she indicated were conversing with Elisabeth and Abigail. The group of girls slowly moved to form a gathering on the lawn.

"You've met my son," Arlene told Josie.

"I have?"

"Yes, Gilbert and my brother's boy, Will, helped unload the wagons into your new home."

"Oh!" Josie smiled and touched Arlene's arm. "What a nice young man. He's such a hard worker. He was so patient with us when we couldn't make up our minds where everything went. And both of them even came back a second day."

"They were pleased with the work," Arlene told her. "Gilbert is saving for a horse he wants to buy."

Constance served tea, and Josie accepted a cup.

"We're delighted that you've come to Jackson Springs," Constance told her. "Our last minister was quite elderly. We all loved him dearly, but for the last year or so he just wasn't up to the job. He's gone to live with a younger sister in Denver now."

"Sam has had only good things to say about the people he's meeting. And apparently he has big shoes to fill."

"Your husband's sermons seem so heartfelt," Vanessa said. "He always has something to say that makes me look at my own situation and try to see how I can apply the teaching. His examples from the Bible give me a perspective I didn't have before."

Josie nodded. "He does have a way of making the Scriptures come to life, doesn't he? He talks about Paul and Peter and so many, as though they lived only yesterday. And Sam strives to use their examples of faith and courage for his own life. I admire that."

Ruby leaned toward Melissa to say, "I always feel better about a preacher man when his wife admires his character."

"It sounds like love to me," Melissa replied with a smile.

Josie's cheeks warmed in an uncomfortable blush.

Constance waved a censoring hand at the ladies. "Josie is our guest of honor and you've embarrassed her. Shush now."

"We're aware that you're newlyweds," Ruby said with a laugh. "Don't be embarrassed."

"Melissa's still a newlywed, too," Vanessa said. "We often hear about Deputy Dan's sterling qualities."

"Likely we'll be sewing little nappies for Josie soon," Melissa said.

"Indeed," Ruby answered. "There's just something about this mountain air."

The ladies giggled.

Josie quickly disguised her feelings of inadequacy and smiled. She couldn't bring herself to deny their suppositions. After enough time had passed, they would stop bringing up the subject in her presence, just the way it had been in her past experience.

Josie had been looking forward to participating in ladies' events and making new friends and being part of this community. No longer was she seen as a widow, nor was she living under a shadow of disapproval. She should have been satisfied, but the women's talk made her feel even more strongly that something was still missing. What was that mysterious extra that these women seemed to have that she could never quite seem to possess?

Josie reined in her thoughts. As many times as she'd read the story of the Israelites and their mumbling and grumbling, and wondered how they could be so ungrateful, she was doing nearly the same thing. Sam had taken her from Margaretta's oppression into the promised land, and she wasn't going to get caught up in being unsatisfied.

The girls had so much fun with their new friends that Arlene invited them to come spend the afternoon at her house. After learning the location and promising to come for them at four, Josie walked home.

It was the first time she'd been by herself in the new house—the first time she'd been alone for many weeks. She ambled through the rooms, touching surfaces, admiring how well the relocation had all come together.

There was so much of Sam's first wife here, from the quilts on the girls' beds to the dishes—and the Bible that lay on Sam's bureau.

Josie didn't mind. She wanted the girls to have those things around them so they could remember their mother. Carrie Hart's belongings were no threat to Josie.

But Carrie's memory—that all-encompassing part of her that remained in their hearts—sometimes Josie wondered if there would ever truly be room for her.

Sam was kind to her. It was his nature. He was even-tempered and generous. And she had more. So much more than she'd ever known with her father or her first husband.

She was grateful to be in Sam's life and to be entrusted with his precious children. This was what she'd always wanted. So why the uneasiness? Maybe she was trying too hard. She was doing her best to be content, so she didn't like feeling that something was still missing.

Josie stood in the towering turret and gazed out at the mountainside. Though she hadn't had an opportunity to do any exploring, the mountain beckoned her. She went downstairs to change her shoes, found her Bible and carried it out the back door. Picking her way here and there, she located a path in the foliage and followed it upward.

The woods tucked their pine-scented silence around her, until the only sounds were the sticks that broke beneath her boots and the occasional scurrying of a wild creature.

After several minutes, she had to stop to catch her

breath. She spotted a bird's nest and a patch of mushrooms.

Pushing on, she followed a deer trail. It came out along an open area that overlooked the hillside and a panoramic vista of trees and rocks, with a purple mountain range in the distance and the town sprawled below. The sight took her breath away.

Stopping on a flat ledge of rock, she sat and studied the scenery. After several minutes the birds picked up their singing. A yellow and black butterfly drifted on the breeze and landed on a coneflower, where its wings beat in a steady rhythm.

Josie opened her Bible to the psalms, flipped a few pages and read one of her favorites. She often tried to imagine how the psalms had sounded when David had sung them. This one was particularly lyrical, and the words so filled with awe and reverence. It was exactly how she felt at this very moment.

"'Because Thy loving kindness is better than life, my lips shall praise Thee. Thus will I bless Thee while I live. I will lift up my hands in Thy name.'" She tried out the words as a lilting melody and imagined a harp accompanying her.

"'When I remember Thee upon my bed, and meditate on Thee in the night watches. Because Thou hast been my help, therefore in the shadow of Thy wings will I rejoice. My soul follows after Thee. Thy right hand upholds me.'"

God loved her just the way she was. He didn't need anything from her except her love and her faith in Him. "Thank you for giving me a family," she prayed. "Thank You for being concerned about how lonely I was feeling. Help me be the best wife and the best mother I can be. And help me not expect more of my husband than he has to give. I do so want to be pleasing to him. You are so generous, and I'm content, Lord."

Josie sang the song again, just to try it out and hopefully so she would remember the tune for the future.

She had forgotten to bring a timepiece, and she didn't want to be late to get the girls, so she made her way down the hillside and back to the house. Turning at the back door, she looked up, but couldn't spot the ledge where she'd perched.

She would find it again.

Each day she rose early to prepare breakfast, make lunches and send her family off to school and church. The days and weeks passed quickly. In the evenings, she and the girls stitched dress after dress while Sam studied by the fire or read to them. She gradually took over helping them with their studies, though Elisabeth refused her help and sought her father instead.

They had settled into a comfortable routine by the time Josie confided to Sam that she'd come down with something that kept her running to the privy. That week Sam cooked and saw to the girls while she rested on the front porch or napped upstairs.

On Wednesday, he climbed the painted wood

stairs after leaving the girls at school. "I was the only father there," he said sheepishly. "Am I being overprotective by taking them every day? They do have the Collinses to walk with."

Josie smoothed the coverlet over her lap. "They love having you take them." Frustrated, she glanced around. "I feel so useless just sitting here." The past two mornings, when she'd insisted on getting dressed and out of bed, he had guided her to a comfortable place and handled the household.

It was probably for the best that she wasn't around the girls right now. No need to spread this any further. But she didn't like the inactivity.

"It's all right to take a few days to recuperate," he assured her. "You've been working awfully hard, and you need the rest. The Grahams have some sort of sickness at their house, too." He headed for the door. "I'll make your peppermint tea. That helps, doesn't it?"

"That will be nice, thanks."

He brought her a cup of tea. "I noticed you prefer the plain cups over the fancy set."

It pleased her that he'd paid attention to something so trivial. She took a sip.

He pulled a chair nearer to her and sat. "I admit I've prayed harder over you than for my sermon this week."

She looked at him in surprise. "I'm fine, Sam. Don't concern yourself about me."

"You are my concern, Josie."

Just as it would be for any member of his flock, she thought. He took his shepherding responsibilities seriously.

"I think we should have the doctor come have a look at you."

"Oh, Sam, I don't think that's necessary. I'm not all that sick. I'm sure I'll feel better in a day or so. Anna's upset stomach only lasted a day."

"Well, this has gone on longer than that. I want to be safe, so humor me."

She gave in with a shrug. "Have you met the doctor?"

He nodded. "Yes." He said nothing more.

"What?" she asked.

"A rancher's young boy was thrown from his horse. I was called to come pray for him, but he'd died by the time I got there. That's where I met Dr. Barnes."

"How awful. Is there anything we can do for the family?"

"I invited them to church. I thought maybe seeing friends would be helpful, but the father isn't happy with God and doesn't want anything to do with the church."

Her heart went out to the hurting family. "I've seen people get mad and blame God when something bad happens in their life. It's very sad."

He agreed.

"You never did that, did you? You didn't blame God for what happened to Carrie?"

He shook his head. "It wasn't God's stupidity that tried to float a wagon loaded with furniture across a river. I bear the full responsibility." He had donned a pair of Levi's that morning, and he sat rubbing his thumbnail along the denim covering his knee. "I was the one all fired up to come west. She would have been perfectly happy staying back east."

How Josie had missed this particular burden he'd taken upon himself, she wasn't sure. His words and expression fell into place, and a deep sadness rested on her heart.

He blamed himself for his wife's death and for the fact that his daughters had lost their mother. He carried the guilt like a cross. "You blame yourself for Carrie's death," she said softly.

Leaning forward, Sam leaned his elbows on his knees and steepled his fingers under his chin. Still, he didn't meet her eyes. "I am responsible."

She sat forward to circle his wrist with her fingers. "You were answering a call from God, Sam. You didn't just set out on a fanciful trip for the sake of adventure."

"Didn't I?" He looked her in the eye then. "How can you know that? The whole idea of traveling west sounded like a grand adventure calling to me. Maybe I did take a fancy and drag them into danger."

She reached beside her for her Bible and opened to pages worn from turning so many times. "Listen to the words of this psalm," she said. "'Trust in the Lord and do good; dwell in the land and enjoy safe pasture. Delight yourself in the Lord and He will give you the desires of your heart.'

"God doesn't just give us any old selfish thing we want," she pointed out. "But when we're trusting Him for direction and doing good, He give us desires that please Him. If you weren't trusting Him for direction, He wouldn't have given you the aspiration to come live and work here. It wasn't a bad or a selfish wish. He called you for a purpose, according to the plan He has for your life. For *our* lives, now."

"But Carrie died on the way. You can't tell me that worked into His plan. Elisabeth stood over Carrie's grave and asked me why God didn't save her mother. I didn't have an answer for that. I still don't."

They sat in silence for a few minutes, the breeze rustling the cottonwood leaves on the trees that bordered the property. A bird called from the woods.

"I haven't told you the worst," he said at last.

Josie couldn't imagine anything worse than what he'd just shared.

"When Carrie was swept away, the girls were screaming and crying out for help. In a split second I made a decision. I had a hold on Anna. I shouted for riders to head downstream and I grabbed Ab and took the two to shore, then went back for Elisabeth where she was clinging to a branch. In that time Carrie drowned."

Josie was at a loss for helpful words. She was grateful to know the cause of the pain Sam had been in all this time.

"I understand your frustration," she said at last. "By your very nature, you're a man who seeks to have all the answers, a man who wants to be able to meet the needs of everyone who turns to you. When you don't have an answer, you feel as though you've let them down."

"I did let her down. I let all of them down."

"No, you didn't. You kept on going. You kept trusting God to put one foot in front of the other, and you continued on."

"There was no choice."

"There *was* a choice," she disagreed. "But you would never consider other options, because of who you are. That man who lost his son had the choice, too, but when something bad happened, he chose to blame God. You chose to trust Him. You've done everything in your power to give your girls the best life you can and to serve the people of this town at the same time."

He studied the tips of his boots for a minute before turning his arm so he could take her hand. "I'm going to go find the doctor. I'm not taking any risks with you."

The tender way he looked at her assured her she hadn't said anything that offended him. In fact, she could almost interpret the tender look in his blue eyes as appreciative.

Chapter Eighteen

Matthew Barnes was a little older than Sam, evidenced by the silver gracing his dark hair at the temples. A handsome fellow, with a ready smile and a startlingly deep voice, he wore a closely trimmed beard and mustache.

"The fact that you get out of breath is most certainly due to the change of altitude," he told her. "You're probably noticing that breathing is a little easier each week, and it will continue to be."

"The altitude never occurred to me."

Sam had seen the doctor to their room, and then left Josie alone with him. "You and Anna may have shared a germ that brought on your upset stomach," he said. "Hard to say, but your continued nausea is easily explained."

"It is?"

"When did you last have your menses?"

"My…" She blushed at the straightforward question spoken by a man, and then reminded herself he was a physician who knew about such things. She directed her thoughts to answering his question. "I don't know for certain. It's been several weeks at the very least." She frowned. "Do you think there's something wrong with me?"

He chuckled and closed his bag. "I believe you're in perfect health. And I think your baby is just fine, too."

"My…" Josie blinked in confusion. "Dr. Barnes, I don't have a baby."

"You will have," he assured her. "In about six more months. Congratulations."

His meaning sunk in. "But that's *impossible*," she told him. "I can't have children. I'm…well, I'm barren."

"Mrs. Hart, you are definitely not barren. You have a baby growing inside you." He ticked off all the signs, and she had to concur she had the symptoms.

"But I was married for several years before my first husband died," she told him. "And we never had a child."

"Then the fault was his, not yours. You, my dear, are expecting a baby."

Josie's head spun with the revelation. Her heart thudded at a galloping pace. "How can this be?" she asked, but it wasn't really a question, and it hadn't been directed at the doctor. "How can this possibly be?"

Josie clamped one hand over her stomach and the other over her mouth, so she wouldn't gasp and cry and fall apart. A gasp escaped her regardless. "Oh, my. Oh! Oh, Lord," she whispered. "A baby. I'm going to have a baby." She grabbed Dr. Barnes's sleeve. "*We're* going to have a baby!"

"Yes," he said with a nod.

"You're certain? There's no mistake?"

"Quite certain."

Visions of a sweet-faced infant made her arms ache to hold her baby right then and there. *Thank You, Lord.* "Thank You!"

A dozen thoughts tumbled through her head at once. Anna's delight. The years of disgrace and criticism from her former mother-in-law. The nursery she'd never dreamed to create, the tiny clothes and nappies. Sam.

Sam.

Other images faded when she focused on her husband.

Sam didn't want more children.

He'd been insistent about the fact that he had plenty to handle with his daughters. She tried to recall his exact words. *This family is big enough the way it is. Babies take a lot of work, and Josie has her hands full taking care of you.*

Anna would be happy, but Josie feared Sam, and most likely Elisabeth, wouldn't share that joy.

Her initial excitement faded into concern. She

had told Sam she couldn't have children. If he truly didn't want any more, he had taken her at her word.

She had disappointed one husband by not having babies, and now she stood to disappoint another by having one.

"Don't tell my husband," she said to Dr. Barnes. "I mean, I want to tell him, so please don't let on yet. Will you do that for me?"

"Of course." Grinning, he carried his bag to the door. "I'll mention the altitude and that you probably just need a little rest. You can surprise him later."

The doctor disappeared through the doorway. Josie washed her face and hands with tepid water left over from that morning and put on a fresh shirtwaist.

A knock on the open door startled her.

She turned to find Sam standing inside the bedroom. "Dr. Barnes said you're fine."

She raised her chin. "Yes."

"He thought you might need a little time to adjust to the climate."

She nodded.

Sam took several steps farther into the room until he stood beside her. "I'm relieved."

She watched their reflection in the mirror as he moved to stand behind her. He wrapped his left arm across her chest to rest his hand on her right shoulder and lowered his head to settle his chin beside her ear.

She watched as he turned his face into her hair, then heard him inhale. He released a warm breath against her neck. "You smell good."

"Sam?"

"Yes."

Her heart beat too rapidly. She ran the words through her mind, and they made her stomach dip with nerves. It was beautiful news. A child was a blessing.

He already had three. He'd married her to take care of them. He'd been confident that Josie couldn't have any. She'd been so sure.

She'd been so ignorant.

"Thank you for getting the doctor," she said.

"Do you want to rest?"

"Yes, I think I will."

"I'll go to the church, so you have quiet the rest of the morning. Unless you want me to stay."

"I'll be fine. You go on about your day."

"I want you to know I'm taking in everything that you said earlier," he told her. "Don't give up on me because I'm hard-headed, and don't stop talking to me when you know I need to hear something."

Straightening, he turned her to face him and raised her chin on one knuckle. His other palm flattened against the small of her back so he could pull her closer. She readily folded into his welcome warmth and strength, where she felt safe. Josie had no reason to deny either of them the simple pleasure of this closeness.

Sam's gaze grazed her lips, his blue eyes sparking fire before he lowered his head and covered her mouth with his. She liked the way he took control of the kiss and framed her face with gentle hands.

Josie craved this affection, reveled in the way he focused his attention on her during their moments alone. The yearning inside made her want to believe this meant he cared for her, but her hesitant, protective side called that presumptuous.

His kiss was tender, yet asked a measure more than any in the past ever had. As he held her this way, while she felt alive and special, her feelings came into distinct focus. She loved him. She was deeply and passionately in love with Samuel Hart. And it was a feeling like none she'd ever known.

Sam ended the kiss and stepped back to offer her a smile.

I love you, she thought, the newfound discovery bursting inside her.

He touched her cheek, as though he regretted leaving her. "Have a restful day."

He left the room and a few minutes later the front door closed. She watched him through the parted curtains on the multipaned window as he took the stairs at a brisk pace and let himself out the gate. Her hand went unconsciously to her belly.

He was doing his best to make them a family and to show her affection. If not consulting with him about the house had been a problem, springing a baby and knocking him off course was a worrisome prospect. Expecting more than he was able to give had never been her plan.

As soon as she could no longer see him, she picked up her Bible and headed for the mountainside. No use worrying, when she could be talking to God.

* * *

Sam had finally laid it all out. His guilt. His lack of confidence in himself. Josie was a good listener.

As he sat in the study at the church that afternoon, he couldn't stop thinking about their conversations, about the way he wanted to share everything with her, and how much better he felt afterward.

In those moments, he realized that he'd never placed all those concerns before God. Of course God knew what he'd been going through, but He couldn't do anything until Sam laid down the burden and stopped carrying it himself.

With the afternoon sun creating splashes of color across the floorboards, Sam knelt and poured out his heart. He admitted his feelings of guilt and uprooted all his inadequacies and helplessness from their long-buried places.

"I regret that I didn't allow Carrie a say in the move," he said. "She went along with my dream and sacrificed everything—even her life. I don't want her death to be for nothing, Lord. I don't want to live my life enduring one difficult day at a time."

God didn't speak to him in a booming voice, nor did a wind carry a dove through the open window, but Sam felt God's presence all the same. Josie's words came to him, words of encouragement and hope. *You've done everything in your power to give your girls the best life you can.*

As he got to his feet, he realized that while his daughters sewed and studied and played of an evening, they talked about their mother in natural conversation. They remembered her alive, and those memories eased their grief.

While listening to them, he'd remembered her alive, as well. He'd thought of days when the girls were small, of the good times they'd shared. And it had been weeks since he'd dreamed of Carrie's death. The images that had been seared in his mind were fading—and being replaced.

Those images were no longer the first thing he thought of in the morning.

Thank You, Lord.

Sam was looking forward to spending more time at home with his family…with his wife. From the beginning, he'd counted on how perfect Josie was for the girls. It had taken him this long to admit—to open his eyes and see—she was perfect for him, as well.

"We got a letter from Reverend Martin," Josie told Sam after dinner a few evenings later. "I picked up the mail this afternoon."

The girls had helped her with the dishes, and he'd carried in wood. "What does he say?"

"I haven't opened it. Go ahead."

Abigail pumped water into the teakettle and set it on the stove. "I'll make tea."

"Tea sounds wonderful, darling," Josie told her.

Sam slit the envelope with a table knife and

unfolded the ivory parchment. "Henry's been preaching on Sundays, and is even able to do chores."

Josie smiled. "That is good news."

"Ned Dunlop attended church with his family."

Josie let her hands fall still on the dish towel and turned to Sam. "Ned? Why, that's wonderful!"

"I'll bet his wife is happy about that."

"I'll bet *God* is happy about that," Josie replied, and they laughed together. "I've been thinking about something. What would you think of hosting a party soon?"

"What kind of party?" he asked as they moved to the drawing room.

"Just a friendly get-together. I'd like to open up our home to the community so they can get to know us and feel comfortable here."

"Are you up to it?"

"Oh, goodness, yes. I'm perfectly fine."

"Well, if you don't think it would be too much."

"It's why we have this great big house. For just such occasions."

"It's a fine idea," he assured her.

She smiled and skirted a chair to gather her sewing basket. He stopped her by taking hold of her hand and tugging until she knelt in front of the fire beside him.

"There's something I need to say."

She smoothed her skirts with her free hand, but grasped his hand with her other. "What is it?"

"I never said this outright, and I need to. I trust

your motivations and I appreciate how kindhearted and generous you are."

She blushed in the firelight. "You don't need to say that."

"Yes, I do. And I need to explain that I let pride get in my way of appreciating this house. I thought I should be the one providing everything for the family. The fact that you could do so much more financially threatened my pride. I'm aware that God providing the means through you is just another way for Him to bless us. I like the house a lot. You've made it a home."

He was surprised when her eyes glistened with tears. Had he been that insensitive to her efforts and her feelings? How many other things had he missed?

There was more, too, things he couldn't put into words, but concerns all the same. He'd been able to share so much because Josie was strong in her faith, and steadfast in her belief that God was taking care of them. He didn't need to spare her by keeping problems to himself. He had sheltered Carrie from difficulties, and now he saw that in doing so he'd done his first wife an injustice. He had no words to explain those feelings.

Footsteps sounded on the floor, and he turned as Abigail carried a tray toward them.

"I only carried the cups, 'cause I didn't want the tray to be too heavy," she explained.

Sam released Josie's hand and took her elbow as she got to her feet.

Josie settled on a comfortable chair. "The three of you are quick learners."

"Did Reverend Martin mention Daisy?" Anna asked.

Sam handed her the letter. "No mention of the cat."

Elisabeth carried in the pot of tea on a second tray.

Josie smiled and poured steaming liquid into each of the five cups. They had just taken their first sips when the front bell rang. Sam stood and strode into the foyer to pull open the door.

"Hello, Reverend," said a tall, dark-haired fellow with a beard. He stuck out a hand. "Karl Stone. Sorry to be interruptin' your evening, but my mother is bad sick. I sent for the doctor, but she thinks she's dyin'—and she wants a minister."

"I'll get my coat and my Bible and join you," Sam told him. "Is it far?"

"It's a spell outside town, but I'll take you and bring you back home in my wagon."

Sam let his family know, and then kissed each of the girls in turn, lastly giving Josie a brief hug with the girls looking on.

"I could come with you, Father," Elisabeth suggested.

He glanced at the clock, noting it was barely after seven. "Gather a wrap and come, then."

Chapter Nineteen

Elisabeth's bright smile assured him he'd done the right thing.

Mr. Stone drove the team away from town, and the night folded them in its inky darkness.

"My mother hasn't been herself in a month of Sundays," Mr. Stone told him. "She loses her balance and forgets things and has terrible headaches."

"That sounds like how Josie described her husband before he died," Elisabeth whispered to her father.

They arrived at a square two-story house with light shining from all the windows. As they approached the door, they heard the sound of glass breaking.

"Mother Stone, lie back on your bed now," a woman demanded in a pleading tone.

"Where is the parson? I'm dying!"

"Karl is bringing him."

They followed Karl along a hallway and into a drawing room. A harried-looking woman with a red scarf tied around her hair was attempting to get an elderly woman to lie back on a fainting couch covered with blankets and pillows. The old woman fought the restraint and jumped to her feet, where she swayed.

Sam handed Elisabeth his Bible and gestured for her to take a seat before he approached the two women. "How do," he said. "I'm Reverend Hart."

"It's about time!" the old woman shouted. "I'm going to meet my Maker, and I want a God-fearin' man to pray over my departing soul."

"I'll start praying right now, if it comforts you," he assured her.

There was a loud knock and a man's voice called out, "Hello? It's Dr. Barnes. You folks down here?"

"We're in here, Doc," Karl called.

Matthew Barnes entered the room.

"Too late for that!" Mildred lunged up and pushed past her daughter-in-law. She bumped into the edge of the tea table, stumbled and grabbed it for support, toppling herself and the other woman both to the floor.

"There's no help to be had!" she cried, flailing arms and legs and trying to roll to her hands and knees so she could stand. "I'm going now!"

"For heaven's sake, lie still!" the younger woman

pleaded. She disentangled herself and leaped away to stand. She crossed her arms over herself and shook her head. Promptly, she burst into tears.

Poor Karl obviously didn't know whether to console his wife or go pick up his mother, but since Mildred was attempting to stand and could at any moment topple again, he went to her aid.

Sam joined him, and together they steadied her and got her back on the couch. She lay back and draped an arm over her face. "Just let me die now. I'm miserable here."

Dr. Barnes inserted himself between the others and set down his bag. "You're not going to die until I say so. Let's have a look at you."

Mildred raised her head to peer at him with bleary eyes. "Last time you were here, you told me to rub liniment into my joints to feel better. Now look at me. I can't even walk."

Dr. Barnes turned to her son and daughter-in-law. "Is it possible she's eaten something poisonous?"

"She hasn't been out of the house, and I feed her well," the younger Mrs. Stone said.

"She gets a delivery from the apothecary a couple of times a week," Karl added. "Her liniment, I reckon."

"Impossible to go through that much liniment," the doctor said. He turned back. "What does the apothecary deliver to you, Mildred?"

"Just my prickly ash bitters."

"Where is it now?"

The old woman waved a hand. "In my room."

"Go get it," the doc said.

Karl hurried upstairs. Sam joined the doctor beside Mildred.

"Damnedest thing to get this old," she said, looking Sam square in the eye. "Don't get old."

Within a few minutes, Karl returned with a lumpy pillowcase. He turned it upside down on the carpet and two dozen or more empty brown bottles clanked into a pile.

"What are those?" the younger woman asked.

Dr. Barnes picked up a bottle and looked at the label. "Her elixir for joint pain." After unscrewing the cap, he sniffed. He jerked his head back and opened his eyes wide. "Seems she's been feeling no pain of any sort for weeks now."

"What is it?" Karl asked.

Dr. Barnes held the bottle toward the other man. Karl sniffed and drew back with a grimace.

"I'd say ninety percent alcohol," Dr. Barnes replied.

"She's drunk!" Karl turned to his mother. "Ma, you're drunk."

"Bring some of that over here," Mildred said, flicking her fingers.

"Make her some coffee and put her to bed. She'll have a nasty hangover, but she'll come around in a few days." The doctor picked up his bag. "Oh, and make sure you cancel her standing order at the apothecary."

Karl's wife looked mad enough to bite nails. "All this time, I've been treating her like a naughty, sick child, trying to get her to eat, cleaning up after her…"

Sam gestured for Elisabeth and they followed the doctor toward the door.

"And she's been *drunk!*" she cried behind them.

They stood on the porch. "Can you give us a ride home?" Sam asked the doc.

None of them laughed until they reached the edge of the property.

Abigail was glum that evening, finishing her reading without looking up from her book, and spelling her list of words for Josie without her usual enthusiasm.

"Is something wrong?" Josie asked.

Abigail shook her head and refused to meet her eyes.

Sam and Elisabeth came home smiling, a fresh out-of-doors scent clinging to their hair and clothing. Abigail immediately excused herself and went upstairs.

"Is it time for bed?" Anna asked.

"You have a few more minutes," Josie replied.

Sam seated himself on his overstuffed chair, and Anna hopped into his lap. He looked at her slate. "You're learning your numbers quickly."

Josie carried in glasses of milk and slices of the apple pie for him and Elisabeth. The rest of them had enjoyed an evening dessert earlier. Once he'd finished eating, Sam ushered the girls upstairs and Josie joined them.

While Elisabeth readied for bed and Josie helped Anna, he rapped on Abigail's door. His voice carried across the hall as he asked her a few questions. Josie couldn't hear Abigail's replies.

After Anna was tucked in, Josie got a sweater and sat on the front porch steps, enjoying the crisp mountain air and the expanse of twinkling stars scattered across the heavens.

Only time and gentle love would heal Elisabeth's heart. Josie understood her need for her father's approval and her desire to be with him. But Abigail's lack of assurance and silent yearning for attention and affection were painfully close to Josie's own lack of confidence. Watching Abigail struggle with her feelings of inadequacy broke her heart.

Josie stood and strolled along the walk. As she'd done constantly, she thought of the baby she was carrying and placed her hands on her midsection. Surely, Sam would love this child, even though he hadn't wanted another. Surely, there was enough fatherly affection and attention to go around.

Gazing up at the broad expanse of sky, she appreciated God's limitless love for all of His children.

The door opened and closed, alerting her to Sam's presence. His boots scuffed along the path, and she turned.

"I was looking forward to an evening at home." His words sounded like an apology.

"You make a lot of sacrifices," she replied.

He told her about the woman who'd been dosing herself with liquor, and she smothered a laugh.

"Dr. Barnes and I chuckled, too," he said. "But not in hearing distance of that poor Stone woman who's been caring for her for all these weeks."

Josie's stomach felt as though it were full of butterflies as she formed her next words, but her conscience wouldn't allow her to stay silent. "Sam. I need to say something."

"You may say anything you like," he assured her.

"You're a wonderful father. You're caring and affectionate and…and *present*. My father was a good man. I loved him dearly, but I never had what your daughters have."

"Your father was a kind man, wasn't he?" he asked.

"I'm sure he was. But he was never home. And when he was, he never had time for me. I have to wonder if my mother felt the same way."

Sam simply listened.

"I learned not to expect much, so that I wouldn't be disappointed. So that I wouldn't feel rejected. It didn't help."

She tucked her sweater around her more tightly.

"I can feel the same hesitation coming from Abigail. She hangs back and doesn't seek time with you the way Elisabeth and Anna do. Elisabeth goes after what she wants and she gets it. Anna confidently climbs into your lap without a doubt of her welcome.

"But Abigail…well, she's reluctant to make the effort, for fear of rejection. And it's not that you're not loving toward her or that you don't include her…it's just that she's less confident of her position. But she's yearning, Sam. I feel it. I recognize it. She needs to be…"

Tears sprang to Josie's eyes and burned her throat. The desire was so real to her—so achingly intense. "She needs to feel *special*," she finished.

And she wasn't speaking only for Abigail. The yearning was Josie's buried insecurity pouring out.

Sam was silent for a moment. "You feel very strongly about this."

"Very," she managed.

"You said something similar back in Nebraska."

She nodded.

"If this is true, if I never saw this, then I've let her down."

"She hides it well."

"*You* saw it."

She felt it more than saw it. Identified. "Thank you for hearing me out. I know I'm not…well…" She didn't finish.

"Not what?"

"I'm new to the family, is all."

Sam surprised her by taking her hand. "New doesn't mean you're not important or that your observations aren't valid. Every day, the fact that I made the right choice in asking you to come with us is reinforced. I need you for this kind of thing. Thank you."

Relieved, she relaxed her posture. "You're welcome."

She was glad he had considered her concerns valid, but hearing that he only needed her for this stung. She was still the same foolish girl yearning for attention.

There were still unresolved issues. A baby wasn't something she could hide. Nor did she want to. She would have to tell him soon.

During the week that followed, Sam asked Abigail to accompany him on one of his calls. At first she seemed hesitant to accept, looking to Elisabeth for her cue on how to react.

Sam had obviously explained things to Elisabeth beforehand, because she nodded and encouraged her sister to go. After they left, the older girl stood in the dining room longer than necessary.

Josie studied her as she held her book to her chest and raised her chin. "You're a good sister," she told her.

Elisabeth swung her attention to Josie. Without a reply, she left the room.

Abigail grew in confidence after that day. She was more open with her father, more certain of her place in his affections. Sam learned that she was good with people. She asked questions, listened when they shared with her, and she paid special attention to the elderly men and women they visited.

Sam was grateful to Josie for bringing about a

change that made all their lives better. He hadn't been used to anyone questioning him, but he needed a different perspective, and he appreciated Josie's perceptiveness. She had felt so strongly about Abigail's hurt, had understood it so perfectly.

Another window into his wife's character opened. She had identified with Abigail, and it made sense, given the times she had mentioned her own father's lack of attention.

Sam noticed something else, too. It became painfully clear to him that Josie was open and affectionate with Anna and Abigail, while she held back with Elisabeth, who was openly resistant to her attention.

And she hesitated with Sam, as well. Sometimes he saw in her eyes…in the way she held herself— that she wanted to touch him…or kiss him, perhaps. But she always waited for him to approach her.

She carried insecurities from her childhood, from her first marriage.… It was up to Sam to make her feel secure. And apparently, he hadn't done that yet.

But he thought on it day and night.

Something inside him, something that had been cold and dead, was slowly, steadily coming to life, unfurling, warming, questioning. What was it his wife needed most? What was it he had to offer her?

As another week passed, Abigail and Josie finished the book of recipes they'd been working on, and Abigail said she'd keep it and add to it always. Sometimes she carried both the recipe book and her drawing journal. Comforted by a growing sense of security and at ease in the new house, Abigail's nightmares became a thing of the past.

As the aspens turned to yellows and oranges, and dried leaves were tossed across their lawn, the Harts put the finishing touches to the house and opened the doors to their community for a harvest party.

"I found this long brass candle lighter in the pantry," Josie told Sam. He lit the wick in the fireplace and then used the flame to light the gas lamps in the chandelier.

"So that's how you do it!" Abigail clapped for her father. "Josie and I were puzzled over that, weren't we?"

"That we were. Oh, look! Our guests are arriving!"

More people had accepted the invitation than had ever been in church at the same time. Parishioners and neighbors were curious about the preacher man, his wife and daughters, and everyone wanted a glimpse at the family who'd bought the big house on the hill.

"I've admired the new colors every time I've looked up the mountain," Vanessa Powell told Sam as he took her coat. She gazed up at the chandelier and then steered toward the drawing room. "I've always wondered what the inside of this house looked like."

"I'll show you around," Josie offered.

Sam turned to greet the Larkens—Victor and

Nadine, who ran the general store, and their son, Dan, the local deputy, and his wife, Melissa, who held their new baby wrapped in blankets.

Elisabeth carried coats to the back porch where Josie had strung rope and placed a rod between two tall cabinets.

The girls' teacher, Miss DeSmet, arrived, and Sam learned her name was Kathryn. She was immediately followed by the Paynes, the Collinses and the Stellings.

Abigail and Anna greeted Libby and Patience Stelling, and the girls disappeared into the kitchen.

A few of the guests brought small gifts, so, after refreshments had been served and people had warmed to the occasion, Sam and Josie opened packages containing fresh canned goods and practical household items.

"I have a gift for the family, too," Dr. Barnes announced. "I had to check with Samuel on this one, and he said it was all right. I'll be back."

Josie glanced at Sam. He grinned and a light-hearted wink caught her by surprise. She laughed and observed the girls who were waiting with interest.

The doctor returned with a crate, covered by a remnant of an old blanket. He set the container down on the floor and stepped away. The blanket rippled.

Anna and Abigail knelt beside the crate.

Hesitantly, Anna reached for the blanket, but a movement startled her and she drew her hand back.

Without further hesitation, Abigail grabbed the corner and pulled away the blanket.

A white spaniel puppy with brown spots and ears and a ring around one eye looked up and sniffed the air curiously.

"A dog!" Anna squealed. "You got us our very own dog?"

Murmurs rippled through the bystanders, and several chuckled at Anna's supreme excitement.

"Can I pick it up?"

"Sure," Dr. Barnes answered. "Your ma will tell you where he can sleep and the like."

Anna and Abigail didn't even notice his reference to Josie, but Elisabeth deliberately avoided looking up.

Anna picked up the wiggling puppy, and Abigail petted his head. "What's his name?" Abigail asked.

"He's your dog now," the doctor replied. "You'll need to name him."

"Let's call him Daisy, like Reverend Martin's cat," Anna suggested.

"You can't call a boy dog Daisy," Elisabeth objected.

"Is it a boy?" Abigail asked.

"That he is," the doc replied.

Libby and Patience joined them, and even Gilbert and his cousin, Will, offered names for the new pet.

Josie and Sam thanked all of the guests for their kind gestures, and conversation resumed among the adults.

Sam sipped a cup of rich black coffee and watched Josie as she spoke with Melissa Larken. His wife looked particularly lovely in her violet-sprigged dress and beaded collar. She had curled tendrils of hair that hung becomingly against her slender neck. He knew exactly how good her hair smelled and how soft the skin under her ear was.

"When are you and your lovely wife going to make your announcement?" Ruby Adamson asked from beside him.

He redirected his attention. "What do you mean?"

She gave him a sly smile. "I've already figured out why you've gathered everyone together."

"We wanted to let the people of Jackson Springs know they're welcome," Sam explained to her. "Josie feels very strongly about opening our home to people."

"Well, then it's simply a convenience that you have an important announcement to make."

"I'm afraid I don't know what you're talking about, Mrs. Adamson."

"Why, I'm talking about your new family member, of course. Some of us guessed weeks ago. Women know these things, Reverend. Why, look at Josie! She's positively glowing."

Sam did look, and yes, Josie was glowing as she held Melissa Larken's baby against her heart and smiled down at him. His wife was lovely, with her eyes sparkling and her ivory skin aglow.

"It's a blessing that you've been given a child of

your very own together," Ruby told him. "Your wife must be beside herself with happiness."

Sam studied Josie again, watched as she handed the baby back to his grandmother, and then raised one graceful hand to her hair in a feminine gesture.

Questions and images shifted through his mind in a haze. Mornings resting on the porch. Subtle physical changes… She hadn't been ill during those days she'd rested and frightened him with her paleness! She was as healthy as could be. And she certainly wasn't barren.

Josie was carrying a child.

At the realization, his knees grew weak.

"Reverend?" Ruby asked. "Are you all right?"

He tore his gaze from his wife to look at the woman. "Yes. Yes, I'm fine."

He didn't know what to think. Why hadn't Josie told him? Didn't she know? Of course she knew. Dr. Barnes had called on her. The fact that she was keeping something so important to herself concerned him. No, it hurt him.

Josie turned and arranged a few plates on the food table. She rested her hand on Abigail's shoulder, and Abigail and Libby carried plates toward the kitchen. Josie turned and spoke to Constance Graham.

His lovely wife was in her element in situations like this. Efficient, industrious, capable. It was when she spoke to him—and sometimes when she looked at him—that he saw the doubt in her eyes. Doubt he'd allowed to take root.

Ruby moved on to visit with a friend and Roy Stelling sauntered up beside Sam. "Looks like all of our young'uns have made each other's acquaintance."

"The girls told me about your daughters after attending a tea party," Sam answered.

"Those females," Roy said, shaking his head. "If it isn't their ma confusin' me, it's the daughters."

Sam grinned. "They tend to have their own language, don't they?"

Roy chuckled and swung his gaze in another direction. "And look over yonder."

Sam followed his direction, to see Elisabeth and young Gilbert engaged in an awkward-looking yet seemingly friendly conversation near the table that held the punch.

"I reckon my boy could do worse than a preacher's daughter," Roy said in a teasing tone.

Sam couldn't think that far ahead. He was contemplating diapers at the moment, not wedding bells. Josie was going to have a baby—*their* baby. He'd been through this before, so it shouldn't have been as stunning, or have affected him as deeply as it had. Was everything all right?

He thought back over the house situation. He'd taken responsibility for not learning more about her and for not giving her the opportunity to discuss her finances with him. What else had he neglected? Was she afraid to tell him? Worried that he wouldn't be happy? He tried to recall what he might have said or not said.

Sam did his best to set aside his concerns and converse with the guests. After what seemed like an eternity—but was actually only a few more hours—he gathered wraps as neighbors prepared to leave. After the last couple left, he found the brass hook and turned off the gas chandelier.

"I'll clean up here if you want to see the girls to bed," Josie told him.

"Where's Gideon going to sleep?" Anna asked, still holding the puppy.

"So that's the name you've chosen. I like it. First we'll take him outdoors and then we'll make him a bed on the back porch," Sam told her. "There's a screen door, so he'll be safe."

He helped her take the spaniel out of doors, and then they found an old coverlet and made him a place to lie within the safety of the built-on porch.

Anna ran to Josie and hugged her around the waist.

Josie stopped her task to kneel before the beaming child.

"Thank you for letting us have Gideon," Anna said breathlessly.

"That was entirely your father's doing," Josie told her.

"But you didn't make him sleep outdoors. And you like him."

"Sure I like him. He's cute."

Anna hugged her again and ran up the stairs ahead of her father. "Night!"

Josie enjoyed the tranquility of the quiet, empty kitchen. She hummed the notes of the tune she'd created for her favorite psalm and sang the words softly.

Arlene and Constance had done a lot of the dishes, so she arranged them in their proper places, took tablecloths out to shake and rubbed a bar of solvent onto the stains, then rolled them for laundering later.

She filled a bucket and had washed a corner of the dining room floor when Sam's heels sounded on the wood. "What are you doing?"

"I'm nearly finished, Sam."

"No, you're *finished,* Josie. Upstairs with you."

At his stern request, she stood, though his admonishing tone puzzled her.

He took the bucket and rag and waited for her to turn away.

"I'm going." She headed for the stairs.

A knock beckoned Sam to the front door. "Miss DeSmet?" he greeted the schoolteacher.

"I apologize, Reverend, but our horse has gone lame. Can you provide us with a ride home? My mother is too old and frail to walk far."

"Just let me tell my wife," he said, and ran upstairs to tell Josie he would return shortly.

Sometime later, Josie had checked on the sleeping girls and was about to prepare for bed, when she heard the sound of a horse on the street below. She glanced out the window, and sure enough, a buggy pulled to a stop in front of the house.

She hurried down the stairs.

"I need the Reverend."

Josie peered out at the man on her porch.

"Frank Evans, ma'am. My wife is asking for your husband to come pray for our boy, Zeb. He done mowed into a nest o' yellerjackets yesterday, and today he's so swollen, his skin's about to pop."

"My husband's not here right now, but he'll be back shortly. Has the doctor been out?"

"Yes'm. Hannah don't want Zeb to die without bein' prayed over proper."

Josie glanced up the stairs. She would tell Elisabeth where she was going and accompany Mr. Evans to his son's bedside. "I can come with you, if it will comfort your wife, Mr. Evans."

"You'll have to do, I reckon."

Josie ran up the stairs and opened Elisabeth's door. "Elisabeth?"

"What?"

"I'll be right back. I'm going to the Evanses' to pray for their boy. Listen for your sisters, should they wake. I'll leave your door open. Your father will be home soon."

"He'll be back shortly," Elisabeth replied.

Josie grabbed her sweater and her Bible and joined Mr. Evans.

Chapter Twenty

Sam returned half an hour later to find the front door unlocked, but the house dark and silent. He removed his boots and silently climbed the stairs.

Their bedroom door stood open, so he stepped inside. Josie must have fallen asleep quickly, though he couldn't see her outline in the bed. He'd wanted to talk to her. He had so much to say, and some things to make up for. He hadn't wanted to wait any longer.

As his eyes adjusted to the darkness, he noticed that the moonlight spilling across the bed didn't reveal a form there. "Josie?"

Surely, she hadn't gone back downstairs to clean up. The house had been dark, though he hadn't looked in the kitchen.

He groped for matches and lit the oil lamp on his bureau. The bed was still neat and unwrinkled. She hadn't come to bed at all. He grabbed the lamp.

The lower floor was deserted, the pail of water standing where she'd left it earlier. Sam went back out, thinking he might have somehow missed her on the porch, where she liked to sit—but there was no one.

After a search of the house, he checked the girls' rooms and their beds. Abigail hadn't had nightmares recently, but she may have cried out and Josie might have comforted her with her presence.

Finally, he set the lamp beside Elisabeth's bed and touched her shoulder. "Elisabeth."

"What?"

"Have you seen Josie?"

"Mama made that sweater for me. Put it back in the drawer."

"Elisabeth, wake up."

"I haven't any coins for your licorice."

"Elisabeth, wake up!"

She rolled to her back at that, blinked against the light and sat. "What is it?"

"Do you know where Josie is?"

His daughter blinked in sleepy confusion. "She isn't in your room?"

"No. I took Miss DeSmet and her mother home, and when I came back, Josie was gone."

Elisabeth shook her head. "I don't know."

"Go back to sleep, then."

She pushed the covers aside. "No, I'll help you look for her."

"I've already searched the house and the yard. I'm sure there's a reasonable explanation."

She accompanied him down the stairs. He lit lamps and stoked the fire in the drawing room.

"There wasn't a note?" she asked.

He shook his head.

An hour passed. Sam felt as though he had a ball of lead in his belly. His unease grew heavier with each tick of the clock.

"She's a capable woman," he said more to himself than to Elisabeth. "But she should have let me know where she would be."

Elisabeth had been watching him pace, stare out the window and then sit and try to relax, as though he wasn't concerned.

"She wouldn't have done anything foolish," he said. "Like going near the mountainside in the dark."

"It's not safe," Elisabeth said, her eyes wide.

"And she knows that," he assured them both.

Another half hour passed, and Elisabeth's chin trembled. "I haven't been kind to Josie."

"What do you mean?" Sam asked.

"I've been rude to her, and I even told Abigail that she was being unfaithful to Mama by letting Josie take her place in our family." A tear trickled down her cheek. "She didn't deserve my meanness. She's always been kind…to all of us."

"Did you really feel that way?" Sam's voice was husky with emotion. "That you would be unfaithful to your mother if you let yourself love Josie?"

Elisabeth nodded.

A stick popped in the blazing hearth, the distraction drawing their gazes to the fire. "I felt that way, too," Sam told her softly.

"You did? But you asked her to marry you and come with us. I thought you had already forgotten Mama."

"I'm not going to forget your mother," he said to her. He got up and moved to perch beside her on the divan. With his thumb, he brushed away her tears. "I loved her. I cherish her memory. I felt like I let her down, let all of you down by bringing you here. By not preventing her death."

"What happened wasn't your fault," Elisabeth said softly.

"I'm learning that. It's eaten me up inside that I didn't have an answer for you that day, Elisabeth. When you asked me why God didn't save her."

"I was so sad," she admitted.

"I know. And I've learned that I don't have all the answers. I'm not the savior of the world. I'm just one man doing his best to share God's love with as many people as I can."

"You're doing a pretty good job," she told him.

He kissed her forehead. "Thank you. I've been doing some thinking about all this, and I thought about what I would have wanted for your mother if things had been the other way around. If I had died, I would have wanted her to be happy. To love someone again."

"Mama would like Josie." She gave him a tremulous smile. "Anna loved Josie right off."

"I expect you're right." He smiled at her. "You know how the Bible says we should all be like little children?"

Elisabeth nodded.

"Children love easily," he said.

"I guess we don't have to stop loving Mama in order to love Josie, do we?" she asked.

"We sure don't. That's the good thing about the way God made us. Our love can just keep growing and growing."

The sound of the front door closing had them on their feet and running toward the foyer.

"Josie!" Sam called.

Sam engulfed her in a bear hug that lifted her off her feet. "Sam!" she managed against his shoulder. "What is this all about?"

"We didn't know what had happened to you," Elisabeth said.

Sam released her, and she steadied herself against his arm. "What do you mean?"

"Why didn't you leave a note?" Sam asked. "Are you all right?"

"I'm fine. I told Elisabeth I was going to the Evanses'. Their boy Zeb was stung by yellow jackets and Hannah was afraid for his life. I prayed for him. I thought you'd want me to, since you weren't here."

"Will he be all right?" Sam asked.

"I think so. Hannah said he hadn't been able to drink before, and we got him to take some broth."

"I'll go out there tomorrow," Sam said. "So you went up and spoke to Elisabeth?"

Josie nodded. "She didn't tell you?"

Sam shook his head. "She often responds while she's sleeping, but then she doesn't remember a thing in the morning."

"I had no idea."

"I'm sorry," Elisabeth added.

"It's not your fault," Josie told her. "I should have taken time to write a note."

"I'm sorry about how mean I've been to you." Her lower lip quivered. "I just missed my mother, and I didn't want my father to forget about her."

The girl's painful admission touched her deeply.

"It's okay," Josie told her. "I understand."

"I was afraid to stop loving her and to forget about her."

"We won't let that happen," Josie assured her.

"We didn't think you would go on the mountain at night, but I was pretty worried when I thought about the animals that might be out there." Elisabeth lowered her gaze to the floor for a moment, and then raised it to look right at Josie. "I love you, Josie. Thank you for coming with us and for loving our family."

Tears rose in Josie's eyes and emotion swelled in her chest. "Thank you, Elisabeth. I love you, too."

Josie took the first step, but Elisabeth threw herself forward, pressing her face against the folds of Josie's sweater and hugging her tightly. The girl's slender body trembled in her embrace.

Looking up, Josie caught Sam's tender expression. He offered her an encouraging smile.

Watching them, love for his daughter and his wife rose up swift and strong. Sam had held himself as much in reserve as Elisabeth had. He had failed to make Josie feel secure within their family. He had made her feel like…a second thought.

He had never told her he loved her.

He did love her.

"I'm proud of you for being so grown up," Sam told Elisabeth. "Come give me a hug before you run on to bed."

His daughter gave him a hug. "Good night," she said. "To both of you. I'm glad you're safe, Josie."

"Thank you, dear. Good night."

Once she was gone, Josie turned to Sam. "We'd better get to bed. It's awfully late."

"We have a little more talking to do," Sam told her.

At those words and his serious expression, she focused her attention on him. "What is it?"

He gestured for her to lead the way into the drawing room, and pointed to the chair in front of the fire. "Have a seat."

Removing her sweater, she draped it over the ottoman and sank onto the seat cushion.

"We have something important to talk about, don't we?"

Josie's heart fluttered with nerves. She didn't want him to be disappointed. She didn't want him to regret any part of what they had together—or his decision in asking her to marry him.

"There's something you haven't told me."

Her gaze shot directly to his. His penetrating blue eyes stared right through her. "Th-there is?"

He nodded. "And I'm pretty sure I know why you haven't told me."

"Why?"

Sam sat on the ottoman at her knees. "Because you didn't trust me."

She didn't know what to say. She held her silence, but her heart raced and the slim thread of safety she'd been clinging to snapped.

"I haven't given you reason to trust me. I haven't made you feel secure."

He was confusing her now.

"You're pregnant, aren't you?"

She thought her heart would stop, but it kept going—chug-chug-chugging away, like a train going up the side of a mountain. She hadn't wanted to let him down.

"Aren't you?" he asked.

How could she have been so naive? She nodded.

"Why didn't you tell me?"

She had to speak around the lump that she could've sworn was her heart, right there in her throat. "I—I was afraid to tell you."

"Afraid of my reaction?"

"Yes," she whispered.

"I remember you telling me not that long ago that

when we trust God for direction, He gives us desires that please Him. Do you remember that conversation?"

"Of course."

"And you desired a family, didn't you?"

She nodded again.

"What about a baby of your own? Was that your desire, too?"

"It was once, Sam. But not for many years."

"You aren't pleased to be carrying our baby?"

"Of course I am, but you—"

"What about me?"

"You told me you had enough children. You said I would have all I could handle taking care of the girls." Her voice broke. "You don't want more children."

"Yes, I said that," he told her with a sigh of regret. "But remember I believed, just as you did, that we would be unable to have children together. And that would have been all right, Josie. I was prepared to be content with our family the way it was. But at that time I had no idea there would be more."

She stared at him. "What are you saying?"

"I'm sorry that you didn't have confidence enough to tell me something so important. It's a shortcoming on my part."

"No, Sam—"

"Josie, if you had felt confident about your place in our family—if you had felt secure and trusted me—then you would have been glad to tell me."

"I trust you."

"No. Trust must be earned. Trust comes from being confident in someone's love for you. You never even questioned the fact that not having a baby wasn't your fault, did you? Remember, I met your mother-in-law, Josie. You've never spoken ill of your husband, but I can guess how you were made to feel."

"I assumed it was me."

"I was willing to be satisfied, but at the time, I had no idea we would create a child together." He smiled. "This baby is no surprise to God. He's not up there saying, 'Oh, no! Now what?'" Sam smiled. "God knew all along."

"I was content with you and your daughters, Sam. Truly I was."

He took both of her hands. "I know you were. But God's plans are always bigger and better than ours. I had no idea I was going to fall in love with you."

Josie worked to absorb those last few words. He'd had no idea…. "You fell in love with me?"

"Think of it, Josie. The Scripture says He knew us before we were formed in our mother's wombs. God knew our child and gave him to us."

"Sam…you're in love with me?"

His blue eyes held concern and devotion, and, yes, they shone with love as he studied her. "I've said all the wrong things, I know. But I took all the right steps, even though my motives weren't clear to me at the time.

"I needed you to help me with the girls. I thought

God led me to you for them. And He did, but that's not all. God hasn't just provided for the girls. He knew I needed you before I admitted it."

"*Have* you admitted it?"

He blinked. "I think—the problem is that you humble me, Josie. There's a peace about you, and you have a steadfast trust in God that I admire…that I aspire to, actually."

"Sam," she admonished softly, wishing he hadn't said those things. Wishing he would just come out and say what she needed to hear.

"It's true," he said. "I've expended all my efforts on trying to fix things for my daughters, while *you*—" he gestured to her "—you've taught them to do things for themselves and you've set an example."

"Our positions are quite different. You carry all the responsibility for them and for the church. You've done a good job at all of it," Josie explained, her voice trembling.

"Everything except assuring you of your place and of my feelings for you."

"If you keep me waiting one more moment, I'll—I will…"

"I love you." He released her hands so he could frame her face. "I love you, Josie, and I'm thankful we're going to have a baby together. I never want you to be afraid to tell me anything again. I don't want you to have a single doubt about how important you are to me.

"I want you as my wife. I want our child. I need

you because you're *you*—not because you are good with the girls or because of any reason except that you are the woman I love."

Sam folded her into his embrace and she rested her cheek against the place where his heart beat.

"Thank You for this wife You gave me to love, Lord," he said. "And thank You for our child."

With her heart full to bursting, tears stung her eyes and a sob caught in her throat. Around it she managed to tell him, "I love you, Sam."

He drew back and held her face where he could look into her eyes. "Say it now."

"I love you," she whispered.

With the fire snapping, he kissed her more tenderly than she could ever remember being kissed. He kissed her the way a man kisses the woman that he loves.

"We'd better get some sleep," he told her finally. "We have some exciting news to share in the morning."

"Do you think we can top the puppy?"

"I'm confident we can."

After banking the fire, he took her hand and led her up the stairs. The answers to her prayers had been realized. For the first time, she truly felt loved and accepted.

Never again would she hold herself back. Never again would she be on the outside looking in, because now and forever, she held her place at the very heart of a family.

* * * * *

Dear Reader,

I'm excited about the release of my first Love Inspired Historical. *The Preacher's Wife* is a story I had wanted to tell for a long time, so I'm thankful I was able to explore this faith journey in a manner true to the time period and to my heart.

Giving my characters' difficulties, and then showing how they react and overcome, is a favorite challenge of mine, and this story was no different. Sam and Josie definitely have to deal with their share of circumstances, from deaths and illnesses to troubled children. I think you'll find their reactions realistic, and I hope you will be inspired by their love and encouraged by their trust in God to take care of them.

I love to hear from readers. You can e-mail me at *Saintjohn@aol.com* and visit my blog, From the Heart, at http://cherylstjohn.blogspot.com/, where I share news about books and family, answer questions and hold contests. I also blog regularly at PetticoatsandPistols.com, the place to learn about all things western.

I hope you enjoyed the story!

Cheryl St. John

QUESTIONS FOR DISCUSSION

1. Samuel Hart was faced with a devastating loss that undermined his confidence in himself and the decisions he made. Can you think of a Scripture that assures us that when we've built our lives and beliefs upon the Word of God we will have a firm foundation for the storms of life?

2. How do you think Josie's relationship with her father shaped her feelings of self-worth? Josie had a strong desire to feel appreciated and valued. What does the Bible say about our value to God?

3. Reverend Martin told Josie she was a woman of great faith. Romans 1:17 repeats that the just shall live by faith. Do we need to have mighty faith, or simply have faith in the might of God?

4. Josie works through the difficult times in her life by trusting in God, reading her Bible, praying and seeing to the needs of others. Have you ever found that when you direct your energy toward helping another, your own situation doesn't seem as difficult?

5. We often pray for guidance or help, but then pick the burdens right back up and carry them. What do Psalms 18:2 and Proverbs 3:5 say about

putting our trust in God? Does faith in God mean we don't have to do anything on our own?

6. When Sam and Josie visited the Dunlop farm, Ned Dunlop was expecting Sam to preach to him or try to convince him to come to church. Ned was surprised and asked Sam about his lack of an invitation. What do you think Sam meant when he said, "I showed you my Jesus"?

7. Sam frequently speaks to his daughters with psalms and verses. Ephesians 5:18–19 says "…be not drunk with wine, wherein is excess; but be filled with the Spirit; speaking to yourselves in psalms and hymns and spiritual songs, singing and making melody in your heart to the Lord." Do you have a particular verse you often use to encourage or comfort? How often are the words of a hymn or praise chorus the first thing you think to say?

8. Josie told Sam it was no coincidence that the Hart family came to stay in her little Nebraska town. Sam agreed that Josie's loving care was no accident. Has there ever been a time in your life that you recognized God's hand in leading you to a particular place or person?

9. Josie finds strength and comfort in reading the psalms and trying to imagine the way David

sang them. Have you ever wondered how David's psalms sounded put to music? Do you have a favorite psalm that you read over and over?

10. Sam felt like a failure because he didn't always have all the answers. What did he have to learn to be at peace?

11. Sam admires Josie for her steadfast, unwavering trust in God for every situation. Do you know anyone like that? Is that you?

12. Though times have changed considerably since the 1800s, do you find it reassuring that the love and mercy of God is a constant? What does Malachi 3:6: "For I am the *Lord,* I change not" mean to you?

13. When Sam prayed for direction, God didn't speak to him in a loud voice. How did he get direction?

14. Sam recognized that he'd been carrying guilt and concern over his wife's death. It wasn't until Sam released those cares that he was able to forgive himself and allow God to heal his grieving heart. Is there anything you've never completely released that has been a burden to you? Would this be a good time to say "I let go" and turn it over to the Lord?

When a tornado strikes a small Kansas town, Maya Logan sees a new, tender side of her serious boss. Could a family man be lurking beneath Greg Garrison's gruff exterior?

Turn the page for a sneak preview
of their story in
HEALING THE BOSS'S HEART
by Valerie Hansen,
Book 1 in the new six-book
AFTER THE STORM *miniseries*
available beginning July 2009
from Love Inspired®.

Maya Logan had been watching the skies with growing concern and already had her car keys in hand when she jerked open the door to the office to admit her boss. He held a young boy in his arms. "Get inside. Quick!"

Gregory Garrison thrust the squirming child at her. "Here. Take him. I'm going back after his dog. He refused to come in out of the storm without Charlie."

"Don't be ridiculous." She clutched his arm and pointed. "You'll never catch him. Look." Tommy's dog had taken off running the minute the hail had started.

Debris was swirling through the air in ever-increasing amounts and the hail had begun to pile in lumpy drifts along the curb. It had flattened the flowers she'd so lovingly placed in the planters and buried their stubbly remnants under inches of white, icy crystals.

In the distance, the dog had its tail between its legs and was disappearing into the maelstrom. Unless the frightened animal responded to commands to return, there was no chance of anyone catching up to it.

Gregory took a deep breath and hollered, "Charlie," but Maya could tell he was wasting his breath. The soggy mongrel didn't even slow.

"Take the boy and head for the basement," Gregory yelled at her. Ducking inside, he had to put his shoulder to the heavy door and use his full weight to close and latch it.

She shoved Tommy back at him. "No. I have to go get Layla."

"In this weather? Don't be an idiot."

"She's my daughter. She's only three. She'll be scared to death if I'm not there."

"She's in the preschool at the church, right? They'll take care of the kids."

"No. I'm going after her."

"Use your head. You can't help Layla if you get yourself killed." He grasped her wrist, holding tight.

Maya struggled, twisting her arm till it hurt. "Let me go. I'm going to my baby. She's all I've got."

"That's crazy! A tornado is coming. If the hail doesn't knock you out cold, the tornado's likely to bury you."

"I don't care."

"Yes, you do."

"No, I don't! Let go of me." To her amazement, he held fast. No one, especially a man, was going to treat her this way and get away with it. No one.

"Stop. Think," he shouted, staring at her as if she were deranged.

She continued to struggle, to refuse to give in to his will, his greater strength. "No. *You* think. I'm going to my little girl. That's all there is to it."

"How? Driving?" He indicated the street, which now looked distorted due to the vibrations of the front window. "It's too late. Look at those cars. Your head isn't half as hard as that metal is and it's already full of dents."

"But…"

She knew in her mind that he was right, yet her heart kept insisting she must do something. Anything. *Please, God, help me. Tell me what to do!*

Her heart was still pounding, her breath shallow and rapid, yet part of her seemed to suddenly accept that her boss was right. That couldn't be. She belonged with Layla. She was her mother.

"We're going to take shelter," Gregory ordered, giving her arm a tug. "Now."

That strong command was enough to renew Maya's resolve and wipe away the calm assurances she had so briefly embraced. She didn't go easily or quietly. Screeching, "No, no, no," she dragged her feet, stumbling along as he pulled and half dragged her toward the basement access.

Staring into the storm moments ago, she had felt as if the fury of the weather was sucking her into a bottomless black hole. Her emotions were still trapped in those murky, imaginary depths, still floundering, sinking, spinning out of control. She pictured Layla, with her silky, long dark hair and beautiful brown eyes.

"If anything happens to my daughter I'll never forgive you!" she screamed at him.

"I'll take my chances."

Maya knew without a doubt that she'd meant exactly what she'd said. If her precious little girl was hurt she'd never forgive herself for not trying to reach her. To protect her. And she'd never forgive Gregory Garrison for preventing her from making the attempt. *Never.*

She had to blink to adjust to the dimness of the basement as he shoved her in front of him and forced her down the wooden stairs.

She gasped, coughed. The place smelled musty and sour, totally in character with the advanced age of the building. How long could that bank of brick and stone stores and offices stand against a storm like this? If these walls ever started to topple, nothing would stop their total collapse. Then it wouldn't matter whether they were outside or down here. They'd be just as dead.

That realization sapped her strength and left her almost without sensation. When her boss let go of her wrist and slipped his arm around her shoulders to guide her into a corner next to an abandoned elevator shaft, she was too emotionally numb to continue to fight him. All she could do was pray and continue to repeat, "Layla, Layla," over and over again.

"We'll wait it out here," he said. "This has to be the strongest part of the building."

Maya didn't believe a word he said.

Tommy's quiet sobbing, coupled with her soul-deep concern for her little girl, brought tears to her eyes. She blinked them back, hoping she could control her emotions enough to fool the boy into believing they were all going to come through the tornado unhurt.

As for her, she wasn't sure. Not even the tiniest bit.

All she could think about was her daughter. *Dear Lord, are You watching out for Layla? Please, please, please! Take care of my precious little girl.*

* * * * *

See the rest of Maya and Greg's story when HEALING THE BOSS'S HEART hits the shelves in July 2009. And be sure to look for all six of the books in the AFTER THE STORM series, where you can follow the residents of High Plains, Kansas, as they rebuild their town—and find love in the process.

Copyright © 2009 by Valerie Whisenand

Love Inspired®

Maya Logan has always thought of her boss, Greg Garrison, as a hard-nosed type of guy. But when a tornado strikes their small Kansas town, Greg is quick to help however he can, including rebuilding her home. Maya soon discovers that he's building a home for them to share.

Look for
Healing the Boss's Heart
by
Valerie Hansen

*Available July
wherever books are sold.*

www.SteepleHill.com

Steeple
Hill®

LI87536

Love Inspired.
HISTORICAL
INSPIRATIONAL HISTORICAL ROMANCE

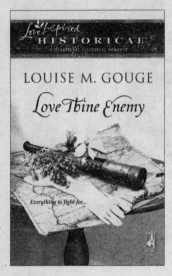

The tropics of colonial Florida are far from America's Revolution. Still, Rachel Folger is loyal to Boston's patriots, while handsome plantation owner Frederick Moberly is faithful to the crown. For the sake of harmony, he hides his sympathies until a betrayal divides the pair, leaving Frederick to harness his faith and courage to claim the woman he loves.

Look for

Love Thine Enemy

by

LOUISE M. GOUGE

Available July wherever books are sold.

Steeple
Hill®

www.SteepleHill.com

LIH82815

Love Inspired®
SUSPENSE
RIVETING INSPIRATIONAL ROMANCE

The Grant family's Sonoma spa is a place for rest and relaxation–not murder! When Naomi Grant finds her client bleeding to death, everything falls apart. Naomi's reputation and freedom are at stake, and her only solace is with the *other* suspect, Dr. Devon Knightley, the victim's ex-husband, who's hiding something from Naomi....

Look for
DEADLY INTENT
by CAMY TANG

***Available July
wherever books are sold.***

Steeple
Hill®

www.SteepleHill.com

LIS44347

Love Inspired.
HISTORICAL

INSPIRATIONAL HISTORICAL ROMANCE

Actress Hannah Southerland's work is unseemly, but her loyalties are strong. When her sister Rachel foolishly elopes, Hannah is determined to bring her home—even joining forces with Reverend Beau O'Toole, brother of Rachel's paramour. Beau wants a traditional wife, which Hannah is not. But this unconventional woman could be his ideal partner—in life and in faith.

Look for

Hannah's Beau

by

RENEE RYAN

Available July wherever books are sold.

Steeple
Hill®

www.SteepleHill.com

LIH82816

REQUEST YOUR FREE BOOKS!

2 FREE INSPIRATIONAL NOVELS
PLUS 2
FREE
MYSTERY GIFTS

Love Inspired.
HISTORICAL
INSPIRATIONAL HISTORICAL ROMANCE

YES! Please send me 2 FREE Love Inspired® Historical novels and my 2 FREE mystery gifts (gifts are worth about $10). After receiving them, if I don't wish to receive any more books, I can return the shipping statement marked "cancel". If I don't cancel, I will receive 4 brand-new novels every other month and be billed just $4.24 per book in the U.S. or $4.74 per book in Canada. That's a savings of over 20% off the cover price. It's quite a bargain! Shipping and handling is just 50¢ per book.* I understand that accepting the 2 free books and gifts places me under no obligation to buy anything. I can always return a shipment and cancel at any time. Even if I never buy another book, the two free books and gifts are mine to keep forever. 102 IDN EYPS 302 IDN EYP4

Name	(PLEASE PRINT)
Address	Apt. #
City	State/Prov.	Zip/Postal Code

Signature (if under 18, a parent or guardian must sign)

Mail to Steeple Hill Reader Service:
IN U.S.A.: P.O. Box 1867, Buffalo, NY 14240-1867
IN CANADA: P.O. Box 609, Fort Erie, Ontario L2A 5X3

Not valid to current subscribers of Love Inspired Historical books.

Want to try two free books from another series?
Call 1-800-873-8635 or visit www.morefreebooks.com

* Terms and prices subject to change without notice. Prices do not include applicable taxes. Sales tax applicable in N.Y. Canadian residents will be charged applicable provincial taxes and GST. Offer not valid in Quebec. This offer is limited to one order per household. All orders subject to approval. Credit or debit balances in a customer's account(s) may be offset by any other outstanding balance owed by or to the customer. Please allow 4 to 6 weeks for delivery. Offer available while quantities last.

Your Privacy: Steeple Hill Books is committed to protecting your privacy. Our Privacy Policy is available online at www.SteepleHill.com or upon request from the Reader Service. From time to time we make our lists of customers available to reputable third parties who may have a product or service of interest to you. If you would prefer we not share your name and address, please check here. ☐

LIH09

Love Inspired®

Whitney Maxwell is about to get a lesson in trust—and family—from an unexpected source: her student Jason. As she and his single dad, Dr. Shane McCoy, try to help Jason deal with his autism, she realizes her dream of a forever family is right in front of her.

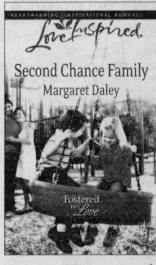

Look for

Second Chance Family

by
Margaret Daley

Fostered
by *Love*

*Available July
wherever books are sold.*

www.SteepleHill.com

Steeple
Hill®

LI87535

Love Inspired.
HISTORICAL

TITLES AVAILABLE NEXT MONTH

Available July 14, 2009

LOVE THINE ENEMY by Louise Gouge
The tropics of colonial Florida are far from America's
revolution. Still, Rachel Folger is loyal to Boston's patriots
while handsome plantation owner Frederick Moberly is
faithful to the Crown. For the sake of harmony, he hides
his sympathies until a betrayal divides the pair, leaving
Frederick to harness his faith and courage to claim the
woman he loves.

HANNAH'S BEAU by Renee Ryan
Actress Hannah Southerland's work is unseemly, but her
loyalties are strong. When her sister Rachel foolishly elopes,
Hannah's determined to bring her home—even joining forces
with Reverend Beau O'Toole, brother of Rachel's paramour.
Beau wants a traditional wife, which Hannah is not. But this
unconventional woman could be his ideal partner—in life
and in faith.

LIHCNMBPA0609